RAZORED

Emmy Ellis

Chapter One

The Guv'nor had folded up his washing and left Lil's Laundrette, pleased with how she'd asked him to go for a drink at the Red Lion tonight after she'd shut up shop. Early, she'd said, because she usually stayed open until late. He'd been surprised by her happy demeanour—

he hadn't expected that at all, considering how he'd up and left her years ago.

He entered his ground-floor flat down by the Noodle and Tiger and hung his coat up, getting on with putting the laundry away.

Reminisced.

Lil could have been the love of his life once upon a time, his feelings had certainly been going that way, but since he'd had an age to mull it over, he'd concluded he'd chosen the wrong woman for that. She used to be *good* friends with Ron Cardigan back in the day, and he supposed he should have steered clear, knowing the old leader would have done anything for her. Guv had worked for him, knew exactly what that bloke was all about. One wrong move on Guv's part regarding Lil, and he'd have ended up dead. His night-time activities going skew-whiff had prompted him to leave the East End and embark on a second life he was now running away from.

He had two daughters, adults now, with a batty bird up north. Hazel, a woman who'd given him more gyp that anyone should suffer. Her screaming matches and outright nutbag behaviour meant he'd left her shortly after his second girl had been born. He'd stuck around on the peripheral, paying child support, taking the kids every other weekend, doing everything right on the surface. Endured Hazel's outbursts whenever he saw her. Put up with a lot.

But it was surprising what you could handle when you had an outlet elsewhere. Something to smooth the ragged edges. Like spying on women. Stalking them. Murdering them if they caught him watching.

He'd done it in London, another reason for moving away when it looked like he'd get caught, telling himself when he'd landed in Manchester that he'd stop it, but compulsions were evil bastards, and some addictions you just couldn't give up, could you.

He'd often thought of Lil. How she'd been his cover, giving him the respectable veneer of a man who wanted to marry and have children, although Lil had never wanted those. They'd ruin her figure, she'd said. Having a partner meant he was someone who wouldn't be suspected of what he enjoyed doing the most. But that last East End kill, it had got a bit hairy, so Guv had packed up and disappeared. Got on a random bus and hoped for the best. Changed his name. Missed Lil like crazy until Hazel had filled the void.

And that northern life had been okay until the last Manchester woman the other week. Similar scenario—if he'd stayed and committed yet another murder, he reckoned he'd have been nabbed by the pigs.

Perhaps he'd been stupid to return here, to the streets that had cloaked him in familiarity as soon as he'd arrived, but he hoped the passing of so many years had dulled memories, helped people forget that after he'd vanished, the murders and stalker reports had stopped.

Lil had called him The Guv'nor earlier, though, and he should have known she would. It was the name he'd been known by back then as Ron's henchman; silly of him to think those who still lived around here would call him anything else.

He cast off the mantle of worry that had settled on his shoulders. Went over his fabricated story, the one that should stop people from questioning him too much after he'd told it. He'd tell Lil later, and as she liked to gossip, she'd spread it around to their old associates, saving him the bother. That's if she still knocked about with them.

He had so much to catch up on. The one friend he'd sworn to secrecy, Halibut, named on account that he'd sold fish on the market, had kept him in the loop, but he was dead now, so London news became nonexistent. At least Halibut had been alive for long enough to tell him there was no more Ron or his sidekick, Sam. They were dead and buried, so the biggest threat no longer applied. Although those little bastards, The Brothers, had somehow taken over. Weird that they'd kept the Estate as Cardigan and hadn't changed it to Wilkes.

Was there something in that? It wouldn't surprise him. Ron didn't think people knew about his Treacles, but Guv did—he stalked, remember. Those twins could be his kids, but Guv just couldn't see their mother, Dolly, falling for Ron's bullshit.

He remembered George and Greg running around as nippers, fighters even back then. He'd often seen them scrapping in the street with other kids. Tell a lie, he'd seen *George* scrapping, defending his twin, letting all the other lads know that *they* ruled the streets.

How had they turned out? It'd be interesting to see that. Them as men instead of the image he had in his mind of them still being boys. It was weird how that happened. You kept the memory of who people were the last time you'd seen them, and when you clapped eyes on them again and saw the passage of time had affected *them*, too, it brought you up short. It had happened in the laundrette with Lil. Whenever he'd thought of her, it had been the evening he'd run. Today, she had wrinkles, although her bang-up figure had remained.

Did she have much to do with the twins? He'd bet George was a nutter. There'd always been something about him, a sharper edge, harder fists, a mad gleam in his eye. To be honest, that kid had given Guv the creeps how he'd stared right through him. Maybe that was Richard's influence. Their dad. But now the thought that Ron might have been their true father had entered his head, Guv couldn't get it out.

Maybe he should ask them why they hadn't renamed the Estate. See how they reacted. If George was tougher than he'd been as a lad, Guv could expect a punch in the face for his trouble, a kneecapping or a Cheshire smile. Halibut had mentioned those.

He left the flat and walked the streets, waiting for that moment when a woman caught his eye, when he *knew* she was the right one, something inside telling him she was. It took a couple of hours, him in his nondescript donkey jacket, beanie pulled low, hands in pockets, until he spotted her in a three-quarter-length wool coat, the royal blue standing out in the drab grey surroundings of Warton Road. Her black handbag swayed by her side, her heels clicking on the pavement. She seemed upset, in a hurry, desperate to be somewhere. Maybe she'd had bad news and needed to go home to the safety those four walls brought.

She rushed to the red front door of a semi-detached, a number sixteen displayed in brass. The house butted directly onto the pavement and, pleased she had a side alley that led to a visible back garden, Guv smiled. Waited for her to go inside, checked the street for Nosy Noras, then nipped down there.

Darkness had encroached. He pressed his back to the bricks next to a window, studying the garden in the gloom. A small patio in front of French doors, a plastic rattan-effect sofa and chairs in black, matching coffee table, glass on top. A postage-stamp lawn bordered by fir trees down the sides and bottom, a nice place for him to hide after he'd seen Lil tonight.

The top part of the window opened, and he jolted. The scent of cigarette smoke filtered out, and it brought on the desire to have a fag himself. Nicotine-free vapes for him now, though.

"I need to tell you something."

Her voice, unless someone else lived with her. And he'd been right in his assessment, she *was* upset.

"Oh God, what's happened?"

This woman sounded fainter, so he assumed Blue Coat had phoned her and put it on speaker.

"Hang on, just got to fill the kettle."

He imagined she still stood by the window, at the sink beneath, so he remained where he was. Water sploshed, then the click of a switch.

"Okay, so I think Pax is following me."

Guv almost barked out laughter at this convenient twist of fate. Whoever Pax was would get the blame if Guv ended up killing her, although another stalker in the mix could bring problems.

I should fix that.

"What? How come?"

"A few times this week he's been where I am. Tesco, the pub, outside Under the Dryer, and before you say anyone's entitled to go to those places, he shouldn't have been outside my work—on *three* occasions. Anyone who doesn't work there doesn't just turn up and stand outside smoking."

"Bloody hell. I knew he was weird, but *that* weird?"

"I should have listened to you. Your intuition is always spot-on."

"So why didn't you, then? Actually, don't tell me. You liked him. You had rose-coloured glasses on. Well, maybe you need to ditch those because the last few relationships have involved creeps and I've been right with all of them."

A doorbell rang. Guv stiffened.

"Wait, someone's here. What if he's followed me home?"

"Did you leave work early or something?"

"Yes, I waited for him to go, then made out I didn't feel well. Seeing him outside again freaked me out. Two seconds."

Guv cocked his ear to the side of the house. Blue Coat could still have her mobile on her and he might not hear what was going on at the front door.

"What do you want?" she asked, her voice coming down the alley. "I've got someone on the phone, so if you try anything…"

"I just want to talk." A male.

"What about, the fact you've been stalking me?"

"What?"

"Don't make out you haven't. I've seen you loads of times this week. I told you my reason for not dating you anymore, and you need to respect that."

"But I thought we were in a relationship."

"I said I didn't want anything serious. Look, in case you need a reminder, this is how it went. We met on an app, dated four times, and that *doesn't* mean we were in a relationship. It means we enjoyed each other's company—until I didn't."

"But you let me meet your friends."

"Uh, no, they happened to be in the same pub as us and introduced themselves."

"Come on, Avery, give us a chance."

"I told you we aren't suited. If you don't go away I'll phone the police."

"What? Why would you do *that*?"

"You're harassing me."

"I'm not, I just want to talk."

"So you said, but I don't. Please don't come here again, or to my work, and if I see you and it's clear you're following me, I'll *definitely* phone the police."

The door slammed, and Guv peered into the alley to see which direction this Pax fella went. He didn't come into view, so he'd gone the other way. Guv crept to the front of the house, staying close to the wall. There he was, a bit of a weedy bloke in a suit.

Leaving Avery to her friend—"Avery," he whispered, liking the sound of it coming from his mouth—Guv went after him. This bloke needed to be taken out of the equation. Incapacitated for a while. Guv didn't need this ponce coming here while he was spying on her, and if Pax couldn't walk, there'd be no problem.

Guv tailed him for long enough that full darkness had oozed into the winter sky, so it must be coming up to half five or thereabouts. Pax stopped at Asif's Corner Store and went inside. Guv waited behind a parked Transit, Pax emerging with a large bottle of vodka gripped by the neck. So he was the type to drown his sorrows, was he?

The rest of the journey took them past St Matthew's church and around the corner to a straight-as-an-arrow street and a slim detached house that stood in a long row of many, again no front gardens. Pax opened a door that might be green or grey—Guv couldn't tell because the lamppost was too far away—and disappeared inside. Opening the six-foot gate between properties, the number on it matching Pax's door (two), Guv investigated the back garden. The opposite to Avery's, it was nothing but a jungle from what he could make out, a thin path going the width of the house, a window and patio doors.

As the lights hadn't gone on, Guv dashed past the window and peered inside through one side of the doors, using his phone torch to get his bearings of the interior. A living room, a tan leather corner sofa, a sideboard, the white walls bare other than a large black-and-white Banksy print on canvas. A coffee table sat on top of a shaggy beige rug.

A door opened at the back in the middle, and a light snapped on. Guv shoved his phone in his pocket to hide his torch beam and moved away from the doors just in time. He peeked round the frame with one eye. Pax sat on the sofa and drank directly from the vodka bottle for a while. He stared at the ceiling, likely thinking about the woman he'd clearly become obsessed with. Then he got up abruptly, put the vodka on the table, and headed towards the doors.

Guv ducked away, flattened his back on the wall between the doors and the window, and hoped Pax came outside. It would make things easier. The door slid across, and the man stepped out to light a cigarette. He stood so close Guv could touch him if he reached out. Pax paused his smoking and seemed to listen. Had he picked up on Guv's breathing?

Pax turned and stared at him, the indoor light penetrating the darkness enough to at least show Guv's outline. "What the fuck?"

Guv lunged towards him, manoeuvring around to Pax's front. He pushed him in the chest, sending the bloke flying backwards, his torso, arse, and upper thighs inside on the laminate flooring, his legs from the knees down outside, sticking straight ahead. Given the height of the doors' bottom ledge compared to the patio, there was a gap under the calves. Guv stamped on one of Pax's shins, and the man roared in pain.

Quickly, Guv dodged round and jumped on the other one with both feet, satisfied he'd broken bones.

Pax's cigarette had fallen onto the floor and rolled to the rug, the fibres catching alight from the glowing tip. He tried to get up, but his fucked legs meant he had no chance. Guv thought fast—he either dragged him outside to safety or shoved him inside.

Inside won.

Glad he had gloves on, he closed the patio door. Pax turned onto his front to soldier crawl towards the interior door. The rug raged now, flames licking up the sofa, spreading across the seats. Guv moved to the window to see Pax better. The man had reached the entrance to the hallway.

Guv left the garden and walked down the side alley. Opened the gate to peer out into the street. It was empty, all the nearby curtains and blinds shut, but soon residents would come home from work, so he had to play this right. By now, the living room would be engulfed, so Pax's exit that way would be blocked. Guv waited by the front door that could be green or grey. If Pax managed to stand on those broken legs it would be a miracle, but in times of great stress, it was amazing what humans could do. He'd seen it often.

A smoke alarm blared, a bit too late in Guv's opinion, so as he would draw attention if he stayed here, he abandoned his plan to shove Pax back inside should he open the door. He turned the corner and headed into St Matthew's, sitting on a front pew as though he needed to contemplate life.

A woman priest or whatever she was approached, and he held a hand up to stop her from coming closer.

"My dad's just died, so I need a minute," he said and kept his head low.

"Of course."

She wandered off through a doorway, maybe to the vestry, and while Pax was more than likely being burned to a crisp if a neighbour hadn't smashed a window and rescued him, Guv waited it out. Had a think. He'd have to ditch the donkey jacket, use his other coat. Stop wearing the beanie and opt for a baseball cap. The priest had seen him, and maybe any neighbours who may have glanced out of their windows because of that smoke alarm.

But the best bit? He had Avery all to himself now, and he smiled.

Chapter Two

Lil couldn't believe she was going for a drink with The Guv'nor, considering how she felt about him. Well, she could, she'd bloody suggested it, but she couldn't believe it because he was *back*. She could have sworn Ron had bumped him off. Lil had convinced herself the old leader had twigged the same thing as her—

that on all the nights Guv had been 'out and about' as he'd put it, he'd been stalking women. Killing some of them. It had to be him, because all that shit had stopped once he'd disappeared.

What did Guv think about her wanting to meet him at the Red Lion? Did he worry she had some bones to pick, that she'd create a scene, seeing as he'd just vanished? Maybe she ought to shock him and not question him about it, act like they were mates, not that he'd *fucked off* without saying a word. She was owed an explanation but would leave it up to him as to whether he provided it. Then again, she knew herself too well, and she might push him for it after all.

Her offer to meet him tonight wasn't about rekindling their old romance, seeing if the spark was still there. No, it was Lil on the road to fucking well finishing what she'd started by killing the bastard in the next few days. During all those conversations she'd had with her friend, Amy, about killing her husband, Pete, Lil had never confessed that *she'd* murdered two men, prevented from doing a third. Guv.

She'd wanted to help Amy because she knew damn well what it felt like to become obsessed with bumping a bloke off and moving on. Plus, it had assuaged the void that had lived inside Lil since Guv had left—a hole only his death could fill. Arranging for Pete to be attacked had pleased her—she'd imagined it was Guv instead. While Pete hadn't died that night, nor the other time Amy had tried to get rid of him, he *had* snuffed it in the end. Days ago at the hands of George who'd shot the abusive bastard in the forehead.

She slipped into her leopard-print catsuit, one she usually had on when she sang for the old people in the care home where her mother had once lived. Elm House was a lovely place, and she enjoyed sitting with the residents afterwards, making them laugh. Mum was dead now, God rest her beautiful soul, and as the twins had bought Lil's Laundrette—George had been very persuasive, put it that way—she only managed it now so had plenty of time to devote to brightening the elderly's lives. She mainly did evenings in the laundrette, although sometimes she covered for Maria and her daughter, Chelsey, who manned it in the day.

It was just Lil's luck that she'd agreed to come in today so Maria and Chelsey could go shopping in the after-Christmas sales in the City. If she hadn't been behind the counter, she wouldn't have seen Guv. But then he knew she leased the shop from years ago, so he might have come again and again until he'd seen her if he was that determined to make contact.

Earlier, he'd said he'd missed her. She'd wanted to snap, "Serves yourself right, if you hadn't buggered off, you *wouldn't* have missed me!" but of course, she hadn't.

She wouldn't have recognised him if it wasn't for his voice. He had a shedload of wrinkles, a salt-and-pepper beard, his curly hair proper grey where it had poked out from under his beanie. His donkey jacket needed a damn good wash, and she hoped he didn't swan into the pub in it later. She'd cringe being seen with him in that old thing. Lil liked to keep herself presentable, and any man she drank with ought to do the same.

She supposed he'd missed her because she'd been damn good to him. Even when her suspicions had come to the fore she'd acted normally, giving him no clue that her blood ran cold every time she saw him after her mind had picked up that strand of truth and weaved a blanket. She'd contemplated going to see Ron, asking him to help her get rid of Guv's body once she'd razored him to death, but come the morning, she hadn't had anyone to kill.

Where had he gone? What had he been doing? Had he been elsewhere in London all this time? Was that why he'd grown a beard so no one recognised him? Maybe Ron had banished him instead of gunning him down. Did Guv even know Ron was dead and the Estate belonged to the twins?

She'd soon find out. She was going to chat shit over a few drinks—knowing her, she'd have to get a dig or two in, but she wouldn't be Lil if she didn't do that. She'd get as much information as she could out of him so she could make plans.

She put the final touches to her makeup, fluffed her black wig. Slipping on her shoes—ballerina style in case she had to run if he revealed his true colours—she put on her latest acquisition, a fitted black leather coat that reached her knees and accentuated her waist with its thick belt. She turned side to side in front of the mirror in the hallway, pleased her figure had remained trim, collected her handbag off the landline phone table, and trotted out of her house, the one she'd lived in all her life.

A cab waited at the kerb—she was buggered if she'd walk to the pub now she knew that murdering bastard was back. Besides, it was cold, and she didn't fancy freezing her tits off.

The cabbie dropped her off in town, directly outside the Red Lion. Despite it being not long after Christmas and money scarce, plenty of people were about, some going to the takeaway pizza place, others to the restaurant or pub. She paid the fare and tip using a card in her Apple wallet on her phone, then got out and approached one of the pub windows.

Guv hunched at the back where Lil had confessed being a murderer to Ichabod, one of the twins' main men. Had that only been days ago? It felt like much longer. Guv had ditched the donkey jacket, thank God, now in a navy-blue suit and white shirt. Christ, she hoped he hadn't dressed up for her benefit in *that* way. Mind you, *she'd* tarted herself up but only to make a point as to what he'd let go.

She pushed the door open and entered. Several people turned round and either smiled or heckled her good-naturedly—"Oi-oi! It's Lil!" She liked that, belonging. Let Guv see she'd continued just fine without him, thank you very much.

She strutted up to the bar, dying to know whether Guv was watching, but she wasn't going to lower herself to look.

Dave, the landlord, gave her a wink. "Same as usual?"

"Yep, but make it a triple, mush."

"Bad day?" He swivelled to pour a vodka from an optic.

She waited for him to spin back round and add tonic water and ice to her tall glass. "You could say that, or maybe it's the best day of my life. Haven't decided yet."

"Cryptic of you…"

"Yeah, well, I like to play my cards close to my chest sometimes, you know that." She jerked her head to the left. "I'm meeting that fella over there."

She wanted to gauge whether Dave recognised him. He'd been running this place for thirty-five years, one of the few boozers Ron hadn't got his hands on. Oh, he'd tried bullying Dave into selling, of course he bloody had, but they'd hit a stalemate. Dave wouldn't sell because it was his dad's pub before him. He didn't bat an eye at Ron's threats, and Ron, in an unusual act of accepting defeat, had backed off.

Bloody Nora, the shit I've seen in my lifetime around here.

Lil got her phone out to pay. "Stick one on the tab for yourself."

"Cheers. I'll have a bottle of lager."

Bill paid, she dropped her mobile in her bag and picked up her drink. Sipped vodka a couple of times to get herself into game-playing mode. Then she swanned over to the table and on her way studied Guv. He'd really changed, so it was no wonder Dave hadn't clocked who he really was.

"Evening." She sat opposite him, her back to the other customers.

"You look lovely."

Ah, fuck off, mate, seriously. That ship has sailed. "Thanks." Coat off, she placed it and her bag on her lap. "So, this is a nice surprise."

Guv grimaced. "Nice? I'd have thought you'd be arsey with me."

"What for?"

"Fucking off the way I did."

"At first, yes, but I've learned a lot since then. Grown up. Realised if you disappeared without telling me, there must have been a good reason for it. Even if it was because life was getting too much—I mean, Ron didn't exactly give you easy jobs to do, did he. Going down for *murder* would have played on your mind, I'm sure."

He paled. "Murder?"

"I know exactly what you did for Ron. Don't tell me you've forgotten I was in the know—and you told me yourself what you got up to, remember. It's all water under the bridge anyway. I moved on."

"But *have* you?"

She smiled. "I just said I have."

"I know, but what I meant was, have you got a fella?"

"No one serious since you. I dabble, which is a polite way of saying I use men for a bit of how's your father but nothing more. Why, thinking of getting your feet under my table again, are you?"

He laughed, although it showed his unease. He clearly wasn't sure how to take her. "I wouldn't be so presumptuous."

"Why not? We both enjoyed our time in the sack, unless you were lying. A bit of fun for old time's sake wouldn't hurt—and I only mean fun. I'm not into relationships anymore." *I wouldn't touch you with a bargepole.*

"Because of me?"

"Blimey, you're a bit up yourself, aren't you? No, as it happens. You know Mum got ill. She ended up in Elm House, then she died. I haven't exactly had the time to get into it with anybody, what with running the laundrette as well."

"All those years on your own, though?"

"Like I said, she was ill for a long time, and I have sex, just not the rest of the shit being with someone brings. What about you? What have you been up to?"

"I moved to Manchester."

She'd have to check the news. See if women were being stalked there. "Ah, right. Nice, is it?"

"It's okay." He seemed pensive, as if he didn't know whether to say what was on his mind. "I settled down, had a couple of kids, although it didn't last long."

"How come?"

"She wasn't you."

Christ alive. He's still giving it all that. "You always were a silver-tongued bastard, but I don't fall for that bollocks these days. Sorry your marriage didn't work out, though."

"It wasn't a marriage. And *I'm* not sorry because she's nutty as a fruitcake."

"Oh dear."

"Hmm." He drank some lager. "Halibut said Ron and Sam are dead."

She held back a spiteful retort: *Oh, so you can stay in touch with Fish Face but not me, the woman you said you loved?* "Yes, and The Brothers run the Estate now. Remember those two?"

"So I heard, and yes, I bloody remember. What are they like now they've grown up?"

"Salt of the earth. George is a psycho at times, but he's a loveable one."

"Thought he might be. A psycho, I mean. He had that look in his eyes even as a nipper."

"I remember he used to give you the willies. They've got this area tight as a drum. They're much better than Ron at sorting things, and no one gets away with anything for long." *So if you're thinking of starting that malarkey up again, you'd best be careful.*

"Know them well now, do you?"

"As it happens, I do." *So take that as a warning that if you're planning to fuck me about, I'll get hold of them to deal with you. If I don't murder you first.*

"I want to catch up with them. I need a job."

"You'll see them around. Can't miss them."

"So you don't have their number, then?"

"I do, but I'm not giving it out without permission. George wouldn't like that. They own the Noodle and Tiger, a new pub a couple of streets away. Maybe you can leave a message with Nessa who runs it for them. She'll pass it on."

"Right." He drank again. "Still living in the same house?"

"Yep." Why did he want to know? Was he going to murder her? "I've rigged the bugger up with state-of-the-art alarms and cameras," she lied.

"How come?"

"Did you not get wind of that serial killer called the Slasher? It was on the national news."

"Oh yeah, I did."

"Every woman around here was scared shitless."

"I thought he only killed prossers."

"Yes, but look at me…" She gestured to her outfit. "I could have been confused for one. Anyway, I wanted to be safe rather than sorry, so now anyone who comes near my gaff gets recorded." She gulped some vodka.

"Don't you want to know why I left?"

"Not really. The past is the past, and you must have had your reasons."

"That's not the Lil I knew. You were always like a dog with a bone. If you got something into your head, you never let up."

Still am if I have to be. "Not anymore. Can't be arsed with winding myself up. I'm all about the quiet life now. I'm fifty-two, as you know. There comes a time when you have to calm down a bit."

"Bleedin' 'eck, you've really changed."

"Haven't you? Apart from your appearance."

He shrugged. "I suppose I have. Hazel did a number on me, so I'm less outgoing."

"What sort of number?"

"She liked to fight, scream, throw things. Domestic violence. I fucked off so the kids didn't have to see it on the daily. If I wasn't there, it couldn't happen."

"How old are your kids?"

He told her.

"You got stuck in soon after you left London, then." She laughed to make out that didn't faze her, but it did in a small way. She'd thought they were going to get married, that he adored her. She'd certainly loved him to pieces—until she'd worked out what he'd been doing at night. "I can't have meant that much to you if you made a family so soon after. Not that it bothers me, by the way. I couldn't give a monkey's chuff to be fair."

"Then why mention it?"

"Just making an observation. What did you have? Boy? Girl?"

"Both girls."

"Won't you miss them, being all the way down here, or is this just a flying visit?"

"I will, but they've got lives of their own. And I'm staying. I've got a flat, thought it was time to come home."

"What did you do for work up there, then? It's not like you could've offered yourself for hire as a bully boy, is it."

"Factory work. Made it to manager eventually." He grinned. "It was shit."

"I bet. How come you didn't come down for Ron's funeral?"

"Halibut didn't tell me until after. We didn't speak that often. Sorry I didn't keep in touch with you or explain. I've always regretted that."

Lil shrugged. "Honestly, I couldn't care less. I stitched up my broken heart a long time ago."

She'd actually suffered the heartbreak while he'd still been living with her, and each stitch had been every aspect of the murder she'd planned. Funny, how they were both killers, if her suspicions about him were right. She'd killed two blokes before she'd got with Guv. Had they been drawn together subconsciously? Had they recognised the killer instinct in each other without actually knowing it?

The thought of her pretending everything was all right, still acting like they were a loved-up couple, brought on a shiver. God, those memories were rancid. She'd been so hell-bent on revenge that she'd been prepared to go through the motions, waiting for the ideal opportunity—but not taking too long in case he killed another woman. Of course, she'd have tied him up and questioned him first, with Ron's help, got the truth out of him, but he'd scarpered before she'd had the chance.

"I actually thought you'd been banished from London by Ron," she said and tacked on a laugh. "Weird what your mind comes up with, isn't it."

He jolted, didn't hide it quickly enough. "Why would he have done *that*?"

"I guessed you'd done something to piss him off."

"Like what?" he barked.

"I don't bloody know, do I! Fuck me, keep your hair on."

He smiled. "That's the fire I've missed."

She smiled back, her mind whirring over how she was going to play this going forward. Tell the twins now or afterwards?

Decisions, decisions.

Chapter Three

Their love affair had to come to an end at some point, but for now, Lil would enjoy it. No one but Ron's wife had the ability to tie him down, and even then that was debatable, considering what he got up to with other women. When he'd approached Lil and called her Treacle a few months ago, she'd been shocked. And had realised the rumours were true. Ron thought the women he'd used didn't talk, and they didn't—they whispered instead, that Ron wasn't the loyal, devoted husband he claimed to be. But who was stupid enough to call him out? No one, so his sordid side remained hidden, only alive in the minds of the ladies he'd used and discarded.

Lil had never expected to be one of them. And she hadn't expected to last this long either. He'd admitted so many things to her, like how Leona wasn't his only child and those little sods, The Brothers, were his. Lil hadn't been surprised, but she'd made out she was so Ron thought his pretence of living a one-woman life was secure.

It wouldn't do to upset him.

Although she'd told herself nothing would ever come of their relationship, she'd hoped to change his mind at first, thinking she could be the permanent mistress on his arm, but sadly, it had become clear that would never be. So she took what he offered, enjoyed it, and wouldn't think about The End until it slapped her in the face.

He'd never hurt her, or threatened her, as if he'd already judged her to be trustworthy. That was true, they'd known each other long enough, drinking in The Eagle, her joining some poker games, and he'd taken it upon himself to be her manager, trying to get her into the big time. It hadn't worked yet, but he'd secured her a few good singing gigs, and he came to watch her on the stage, looking proud, like he'd created her.

No, the talent was all hers, she'd never let him claim that.

She made sure Mum had everything she needed for the evening, snacks close by, a Thermos filled with tea. Mum and her telly marathons were legendary in this house, and she only got up to got to the loo between programmes.

Lil kissed her on the cheek.

"You're meeting him *again, aren't you," Mum said from her favourite chair, sounding disgruntled that Ron was once again coming to pick her daughter up. Mum's dislike for him seemed bone-deep, but she'd never said why.*

Lil sighed. "Yes."

"You need to watch yourself. He's a user. He'll throw you away when someone else comes along. Plus people will talk."

"Why? No one knows it's him, and it's not as if we go anywhere people round here would spot us."

"Still into wearing his disguises, is he? And it's all a bit sordid, love, him choosing you. Bloody gross, in fact. I wanted more for you than him. He's…not a nice man."

"Yeah, but maybe I'm not the type to get more. I have to accept my lot and be happy with it."

"There are so many nice men out there..."

"But none of them are exciting."

"Dangerous, more like." Mum sighed. "Go on, off you go. And be careful. Don't trust a word that comes out of his mouth."

Lil nodded and moved to the window, parting the curtains a crack to peer outside into the night. There he was, in a wig and beard, sitting in a stolen car, the plates switched to fakes. This was what he did, how he went about in secret with her. In that getup he was someone else, albeit still with his air of menace, but not half as bad as the Ron everyone else got to see.

"He's here. Tarra!"

She left the house, anticipation of what was to come whipping through her. A parcel had arrived earlier, containing the red dress she had on. Mum had taken it off the step; Lil had been at work in the laundrette. She leased it, and Ron had given her money for all the machines. One day she planned to buy the building.

She got in the passenger seat and stared forward, as per instructions, and Ron drove away, Lil mindful that people would be assuming she was picked up by a different man each week, all the cars different, too, except it was Ron each time. They'd think she was a slag, but what did she care? She was young and carefree, and so far, the year was shaping up to be the best yet. She had Ron and his gifts, and her business was booming. What more could she ask for?

A career on the stage, that's what.

She had no bookings this weekend, so no rendezvous in a hotel afterwards and the freedom of being completely themselves without fear of anyone seeing them. It thrilled her, this affair.

"Where are we going tonight?" she asked.

"I thought we'd get pissed up in this place I own. There's somebody there, a man I want you to see."

Her heart leapt. Was it a bloke from a record company? Had Ron finally come through on his promise? Mum said she'd take over the laundrette if Lil became a star, so there was nothing to worry about there.

"Sounds exciting."

"For me and you, yes, but not so much for him."

That didn't sound right, but hope continued to bloom anyway.

Ron drove away from her housing estate and eventually came to a dark track in a rural area. He turned down it, the car jostled by deep ruts, branches scraping the sides. It was like a tunnel, the tree foliage meeting overhead, an archway of thick leaves, the moon peeking through. This should scare her, being taken somewhere so remote, but she trusted Ron, believed they had something so special that he'd never hurt her.

He veered right at the end into a forest area, and the headlights picked out a small white-stone cottage, although the windows had been boarded up with steel panels, as had the front door, but it had a keyhole. She imagined it was a love nest, something he'd bought just for them.

"What's this all about?" she asked.

He parked and shut off the engine, plunging them into darkness. "I bought this originally to do it up and sell it, but you know how dark my mind is, so I decided to refurb it to certain specifications. Took me a fair old while, coming here when I got the chance, a bit of DIY here and there. Hid behind the guise of a shell company and paid some bloke from one of my offshore accounts to put all that steel up and do a few bits and bobs inside."

"So he doesn't know who you are. Clever."

"Yeah, that's me." He paused and reached over to hold her hand. "I want you to have it. I've put it in your name. It can be a bolthole, somewhere for you to come if shit gets too hard. Plus, you don't want to live with your mum forever, do you?"

"Err, how about no?" But in truth, Lil wouldn't mind staying with Mum. They got along well, but she knew what he meant. She had to spread her wings sometime. She wasn't sure she wanted to do that in the middle of nowhere, though.

He laughed. Sobered. Got a set of keys out and handed them to her. "There's a room inside that I keep locked. I'll need to use it from time to time, okay?"

"Okay…" She popped the keys in her bag. "Thank you. For this. Do I need to keep the steel over the windows?"

"Until I stop needing that little room, yeah. When I was younger, before I got my army together and became who I am now, I loved the one-on-one interactions with people who'd pissed me off. Slapping them about, giving it a load of verbal, all that. I've missed it, so I go back to it from time to time. No one knows, not even Sam."

Sam, the lumbering right-hand man who was so devoted to Ron he was blinded by it. The man would do anything he asked, and a lot of people secretly took the piss out of him because he seemed dumb half the time.

"But now you *know," Ron said. "And it's easy, to say what I need to in the dark, when I'm pretending*

I'm not who I really am, because the dark has a habit of protecting you, doesn't it."

"What are you trying to say?"

"It's getting dangerous, me and you."

"Shit, has someone twigged we're seeing each other?"

"Nah, nothing like that, Treacle. It's me, my feelings. See, there's something about you, you've got under my skin almost as much as my wife, and that's saying something. She's my perfection, the woman I should revere above all others. I shouldn't shag about behind her back, she doesn't deserve it, yet I still do it. I separate her from everything else. When I step inside my house, she's all I see. A bit like with you. When we're together, no one else exists, not even her. That's why it's dangerous."

Jesus, was he saying what she thought he was saying?

"If I let you get any deeper inside me, things could come crashing down, know what I mean?"

"I think so." He was going to end it, she knew it. "I… You know I'll never say anything, don't you."

"Yeah. We're not here for me to kill you, so stop worrying. I've got no intention of bumping you off. Here's the thing. There's a side of me that only my wife sees, she owns that part of me, and no one else has ever

come close until you. You own another part, though. You're a bewitching little trollop, and all the others—and there have been plenty—they've never made me feel much beyond wanting to shag them, control them, be a cruel bastard. I'm falling for you, plain and simple, and it's gone too far already. I'm going to have to let you go. But I'm telling you now, the bond is too deep for me to just walk away completely. I still want to see your face every now and then. Watch you singing."

"I never thought it would even last this long, so…"

He laughed. "Me neither. I want you to know that if anyone hurts you, tell me and I'll end them. I want you to see inside this place and know you're the only other person who's seen it—other than…well, you'll get the gist in a bit."

Tears prickled, and a lump sat in her throat. "You said you wanted me to see a man. Is he inside?"

"Yeah. I listened, you know, to everything you've ever told me."

"What do you mean by that?"

"You'll see. Come on, there's some nosh and booze indoors. We'll stay overnight, make the last hurrah a good one."

So this was it, the final time, and all because he loved her. She wished he didn't, but then again, she'd never have lasted this long otherwise. It seemed inconceivable, him caring for her like that, but she should have cottoned on when he'd helped her with the laundrette, not asking for protection money or taking any repayments for the machines.

Yes, she should have known.

And now she did.

He kissed her then, tender, and she stared at him in the darkness, sealing the sight of him inside her head forever. No one else knew this side of him, the side he showed her. He was a million personalities, and she was grateful he'd given her one of the nicer ones.

Tears fell, and he wiped them away with a thumb, his skin rough on her cheek.

"I'll set you up with someone else," he said. "Someone I trust."

She nodded, knowing she didn't have a choice.

Metal manacles clung to the man's wrists, pinching tight. Chains held him up, attached to a winch in the ceiling, and a steel wire went from there to a thing on the wall. A handle—was that turned to hoist him up? Naked, he stared at Lil, one eye black, swollen shut, and the awful, awful realisation of who he was gnawed at her soul.

Ron had indeed listened to everything she'd told him.

Steel encased the room, creating a metal box. The floor had a trapdoor in it, currently open, a nasty smell wafting up. In the harshness from the spotlight trained on the man, she made out shapes in the murk below—a body, perhaps, or maybe that was two. Faces, one with its cheek missing where rats must have had a good chew or someone had sliced it off.

"I found him," Ron said. "Like I said I would."

Lil couldn't believe this. "You did, although I told you not to worry about it."

The hanging man had hurt her many years ago when they'd been fifteen. It was still raw, as first-love endings tend to be, and she'd said to Ron that there was no need to 'round him up and a kill the fucking bastard' because of the fact they'd been kids. Children made mistakes. Simon, beaten black and blue, didn't really deserve to be here. Ron wouldn't have seen it like that, though. He'd say Simon needed to pay for what he'd done, but Lil would prefer he be set free. This…this torture was enough.

"Will you be letting him go?" she asked.

"Nah, rapists don't get a free pass."

While the law classed what Simon had done as rape—and it absolutely was, because Lil had said the required no—she didn't quite see it like that. It was the first time for both of them, and it had hurt, that point when Simon had tried to break the barrier inside her. She'd asked him to stop, but he'd pressed in some more. After that she'd stayed silent, crying from the pain of the in-and-out motions, wishing she was one of those girls who 'didn't feel a thing' when their virginity was taken.

She reckoned those girls were lying.

Simon had become too excited, that was all. Lust had taken over, or whatever the hell happened to fifteen-year-old boys, and rape was such a strong word, wasn't it? Or was Lil guilty of trying to make this 'less than' so she could cope with it better?

"Please," Simon whispered. "Please…"

Ron's answer was to lop off his cock using one of the knives from the kitchen. It plopped into the darkness below. Simon screamed so loud it hurt Lil's ears. She swallowed—the sight of all that blood pissing out of the stump brought on nausea, and she was in danger of losing the nice steak dinner Ron had cooked for her, not to mention the whole bottle of red wine she'd had to herself before he'd brought her in here.

"The key to coping with harsh memories is remembering, over and over, what the person did when they hurt you," Ron said. "It breeds vengeance, a fucking swarm of it, and it's fuel to keep you going. Whenever life gets too tough, concentrate on all the evil things you could do to them. Think about it, imagine killing whoever pissed you off, because believe me, it helps. In my case, I actually kill them, but I wouldn't recommend you do that unless you come to me first, understand?"

A touch of the 'other' Ron had crept in, the hardman, the one who had no time to love a woman like her. All business.

Simon choked on his tears. "I swear to God, please, let me go…"

Ron stepped up and, blade at Simon's neck, swiped to the right.

Lil looked away. The chains rattled—Ron taking off the manacles?—then came a thud where Simon must have landed on whoever else was down below. She left the steel box, passing the living room that gave the impression this place was normal, a cosy nook for lovers. She popped her head into the bedroom, so obviously a male's domain. In the bathroom, she washed her face, didn't care that her makeup would come off. Ron had seen her without it plenty of times.

She entered the kitchen, getting on with cleaning up the plates, stacking them in the dishwasher along with everything else Ron had used to cook. Their meal, in such a private setting, had given her an insight into what it would have been like to live with him. But it was a sheen of lies. She'd have to put up with him coming home at all hours, barely seeing him, and knowing he had other Treacles sitting on his lap, despite him loving her.

She sat at the table with a coffee, not interested in what Ron was doing to Simon's body in the crawl space beneath that strange little room. She had a future to live without him, so she may as well get used to his absence now.

Chapter Four

Guv had left the pub, swapping numbers with Lil and promising they'd get together again soon. On his walk towards Pax's street, he inspected the evening's conversation. Lil was the same but not. He couldn't put his finger on the change, but he hadn't expected her to not care that he'd left her. For years he'd imagined her harbouring a massive grudge, but it seemed she'd put it all behind her. She must have, to sit and chat with him like nothing had happened. It jumbled up the scenario he'd planted firmly in his mind. How stupid of him to have thought she'd be the same girl he'd planned to marry. Of *course* she'd be fucking different.

He was chuffed she hadn't had any serious relationships since him, though. No matter what she'd said, it meant she'd loved him more than anyone else—he was the one who'd got away. The same could be said for him regarding her; in Manchester, he'd had to force himself to forget Lil and set up home with Hazel. Chop Lil out of his head and heart for the most part.

He should have told her he was leaving, though, something he regretted not doing. The two men she'd been involved with previous to him had walked out on her without a word, too, and he'd known him doing the same would have wounded her. She hadn't even batted an eyelid when he'd said he'd kept in contact with Halibut. He'd done that for a couple of reasons. One, to keep tabs on the whispers around Cardigan about the stalker going quiet, and two, to find out what Lil was up to, although Halibut was useless in finding anything out about her other than she still drank in the Red Lion and continued to run the laundrette.

He stopped at the end of Pax's street, close to the house. A crowd stood talking, mostly women in thick dressing gowns and slippers, arms folded to ward off the cold. The house itself, a burned-out shell, seemed to mourn the loss of its windows where they must have blown out. At least it was a detached so it hadn't affected the neighbours either side.

Guv walked closer. "What the hell's happened here, then?"

"No idea whether it's arson or what yet," a blonde lady said, her hair basted by the light from the streetlamp. "The fire engine's only just gone; they were here ages because embers kept cropping up. The wotsit's here tomorrow, the one who works out how it happened. But the fella who lived there couldn't get out."

"Dead, then?" he asked.

"What do *you* fucking think? If a house is on fire and I said he couldn't get out..."

Guv had forgotten how the women round here could be. Snappy. Big-mouthed. "Sorry, wasn't thinking."

"Obviously not."

"Who was the bloke?"

"Pax Shaw. Young. Did you know him?"

"No."

Guv wandered off. This would make the local news, so Avery was bound to hear about it at some point. Seeing as the cigarette had caused the fire, it would likely be put down to an accident, but those broken legs… Guv would need to be careful. With Pax dead, there was no one to blame the stalking on.

He strolled to her road, conscious he didn't have a beanie on, his donkey jacket. But he was grey-haired now, so no one would suspect he was dodgy, thinking him some random old man, although fifty-odd wasn't bloody old. When imagining stalkers, people tended to conjure up dark clothing, and although his suit was navy, his white shirt wasn't exactly pervert material, was it.

He checked the windows as he casually strolled down her street. Curtains closed, no one about. Wheelie bins sat at the kerbs. They hadn't been there earlier, so tomorrow must be rubbish day. He dipped down the side of her house and crept to the back. Light painted squares on the grass from the panels in the French doors, but the blind over the window was down. Sidling along to the left, he peered round the frame.

A laptop on a dining table, open. A cup next to it with steam curling from it. Half a glass of juice in front of another chair. But no Avery in that side of the room. He poked his head out farther so he could check the kitchen to the right. In a dressing gown the same blue as her coat, she stood with her back to him at a wall cupboard containing snacks. Quickly, he skirted beyond the light squares on the grass and darted to the fir trees, wedging himself between the two closest to the house, the perfect spot to see the whole room bar the sink area beneath the window.

She sat at the table with a packet of crisps, slinging another bag that came to rest by the juice. Did she have a guest? Yes, a woman entered in pink Barbie pyjamas and sat. Their mouths moved, but he couldn't lip-read so had no idea what they were on about. Avery stood, took a packet of cigarettes out of her dressing gown pocket, and came towards the doors. Opened one a slice.

Thank you, God.

She lit up, blowing smoke outside. She'd been crying, eyes puffy and red, the tip of her nose scarlet. Maybe she'd heard about Pax, but why would she be upset? Four dates wasn't exactly enough to get attached to someone, was it? And anyway, she'd said she didn't want a relationship with the bloke, so what the hell?

He'd never understand women.

"I can't stop thinking about how he must have felt," she said. "It would have been so *hot*. Can you imagine burning to death?"

"No, it doesn't bear thinking about." It was the same voice as the woman on the phone earlier.

Was she Avery's sister? They looked similar, but he'd noticed many young women did these days, all following the lip-pout route and those godforsaken eyebrows. As she was in pyjamas, she might pose a problem. She could be staying here for a while. That would fuck with what Guv usually did—going into the house when his targets were asleep and moving things around to mess with their heads. Whatever he did tonight would be blamed on that other woman and vice versa.

"I dread to think what his parents are going through." Avery took another drag of her cigarette. "What if he set the fire on purpose because of what I said to him? What if he killed himself?"

Ah, so that's why she was crying. Guilt.

"Look, you weren't to know he was as unstable as that. Okay, you thought he was a bit weird up top, but not to that degree. If he can't handle someone telling him he's not right for them, then that's not your fault. People date on apps all the time, and loads don't get past the first date. You don't see them starting fires, do you. I *have* wondered why you went on four, but..."

"He wasn't weird until the last one. Talking about us getting married and having kids as if we'd been seeing each other for ages. Like it was a given. It was too much too soon. I don't understand why he didn't get that."

"Next time, don't tell them your address unless you're one hundred percent sure they're okay. Him coming round earlier...a bit bloody much, wasn't it?"

Avery nodded. Stared into the garden in his direction. Could she see the tree branches had been disturbed? See him? Guv placed a hand over his mouth, cupped, so his breath didn't cloud and filter out in the cold air.

"Actually," the guest said, "stop using apps and meet someone in the pub instead. I've never liked the fact you don't know these people and just turn up for the first meet at a restaurant and hope for the best."

"Maybe." Avery finished her cigarette and closed the door.

How long were they going to sit there chatting? Guv cursed himself for not putting his coat on over the suit. It was bloody cold, and he might have to stand here for a while. He did remember his gloves, though, so that was something.

The women remained until the drinks and crisps were gone. Avery closed the laptop, and they rose. The guest went to pick the cup and glass up, but Avery waved as though to tell her to leave it until the morning. A "No" spoken, going by the shape of her lips, so it was something they'd both remember when they woke up.

Guv smiled as they left the room, the light going off.

Neither of them had locked the door.

He waited for twenty minutes, all he could stand; he shivered from the chill and rubbed his arms, then stepped out from the trees. No security light snapped on, which was stupid, considering Avery lived alone—or did she? The 'guest' might actually be a housemate. He'd never messed with two people in one place before, so this might be interesting.

He entered the dining area, closing the door quietly behind him. Picked up the cup and glass going from memory and crept over to the sink. Put them in the washing-up bowl. A splosh indicated water was already in there, so he swilled them out and put them on the draining board upside down. Annoyed his leather gloves had got wet, although the water hadn't penetrated to his fingers, he took his phone out and accessed the torch app, turning the intensity of the beam down. At the hallway door, he glanced up by the stairs—no lights on. No sound or movement.

He found the living room at the front. Greenish-yellow light from an Alexa flashed—she was listening—and he smiled. Leaned close to it and said, low, "Alexa, play creepy music."

"Okay, playing creepy music."

He exited the house to the sounds of a shriek above and a strange tinkling melody.

They'd smell his aftershave. They'd see he'd washed up. They'd know someone had been in the house. They'd check the back door and find it unlocked.

Silly, silly girls.

Chapter Five

Switching on the hallway lights top and bottom then racing downstairs, Avery shouted, "Alexa, shut up!" The weird, spooky music continued, and she poked her head into the living room and repeated the instruction. The racket stopped, and she sighed with relief. Alexa didn't do things randomly on the regular, but this had happened a few times before, albeit in the day. The only reason Avery shook now was because it was late at night and she'd been startled awake.

Louise came halfway down the stairs and bent over the banister rail. "What the fuck?"

"I know. I didn't think those things were supposed to come on unless you said her name." Avery wandered into the kitchen. She was wide awake now, thanks to the shock, and may as well make some tea. She frowned. "Did you spray deodorant when you had your shower before bed?"

"No."

"Perfume?"

"No."

"I can smell something." She stared at the sink. "Did you wash the cup and glass?"

Louise came in and stood behind her, staring at the draining board. "No…"

"Well, *I* didn't do it." Avery spun to face Louise, her skin going cold. "What if someone…?"

"Oh, don't say that."

Avery ran to the French doors and yanked the handles just to put her mind at rest. They moved down, and the doors opened. "Oh fuck, I didn't lock up after I had my fag." She slammed the doors shut and secured them, wrenching the curtains across. "Someone's been in here?"

Louise blinked rapidly. "What, and washed up? What kind of weirdo does *that*?"

Avery brushed past her and dashed into the hallway to inspect the front door. The chain was on, the bolts across, so no one had come and gone that way. She returned to the kitchen. "Are you *sure* you didn't wash them? Are you messing about, trying to scare me?"

"I swear, it wasn't me."

"I'd have blamed Pax if he wasn't dead."

"We'd better look round the rest of the house."

"There's only the bathroom we haven't seen."

They went upstairs, Avery going first. If someone was up there, she didn't know what the hell she'd do. And if there wasn't, phoning the police and saying someone had walked in via the unlocked doors and washed up a cup and glass would sound bloody ridiculous. She pushed the bathroom door. No one stood in the glass shower cubicle, so she poked her head around. No one sitting on the toilet.

Had the person asked Alexa to put that music on, or was that just a coincidence? Avery hadn't washed up, and she believed Louise hadn't, so who the fuck had?

"I can't go back to bed now, not after that."

"We'll sleep on the sofas, all right?"

Louise collected their quilts and pillows, and Avery went back down to make them a cuppa. She kept glancing over at the French doors expecting someone to jump out from behind the curtains. The sight of the cup and glass on the draining board, and the fresh water that had come off them, meant whoever had been in here had only just washed them, didn't it?

She took the teas into the living room and settled down on a sofa. What with Pax dying in that fire and now this, she was a bag of nerves. "I can't stop thinking about someone being in here."

Louise sighed. "*And* why they'd wash up then leave—or put that music on and leave."

"Do you think Pax told a friend about me, and now he's dead they came round to shit me up me or something?"

"I don't know, but it's bloody odd."

Avery prepared herself for a night of no sleep. "Should I phone the police?"

"Might be best to get a log of it. Did you notice if anything had been taken?"

"Fuck, my laptop!" Avery put her cup on a side table and bolted to the kitchen.

The laptop was still on the table.

What the hell?

Chapter Six

At ten in the morning, George and Greg Wilkes stood in the new hair salon they'd purchased. The sign for Curls and Tongs would be put up later, and Stacey had agreed to be a manager for them. This place added to the other going concerns they owned that acted as a cover for their dodgy shit.

“What do you reckon?” George asked Stacey, who they’d met a few days ago by helping to capture her ex, Joe Osbourne.

“It’s perfect,” she said. “Everything’s already here.”

“Yep, included in the sale price, so you should be able to open up pretty quickly once you’ve found your staff.”

“Oh, so you’re not doing that?”

“No, we might be the ones owning it, but everything else is down to you, as if you’d bought it. That’s what you wanted, isn’t it?”

She nodded.

Stacey could afford to buy this herself, she had six hundred thousand in cash, her half of what had been shared between herself and Hailey, Joe’s girlfriend. But the money had come from the sale of drugs, and she had no proof she’d earned it, so it was better that she didn’t use it for big purchases. The twins had yet to discover the county line their new copper, Bryan Flint, had been infiltrating undercover. It seemed the gang had been tipped off and moved elsewhere, because the only drug pushers on Cardigan were those George and Greg allowed.

Always suspicious, George worried that Flint had been the one to give the gang the nod, but as he couldn't prove it, he'd keep his mouth shut for now. It was early days, Flint had only just done his initiation by killing Joe on Saturday, and they hadn't had the chance to set him in action as their dodgy copper. Their present one, Janine, would be leaving them soon as she'd got herself up the duff. She'd been teaching Flint the ropes, and hopefully she would give the go-ahead that he was able to fly on his own soon.

Thankfully, they'd had no need of police database searches in the last few days, so Janine was likely enjoying the downtime and Flint had yet to be roped into anything else. All was quiet on Cardigan, which made a change, and Greg had been able to spend a lot of time during the day with Ineke, the woman they'd rescued from Amsterdam. Greg was taking it slowly, getting to know her, which George thought was sensible. Ineke had been through a lot, and Greg didn't want to stress her.

Stacey smiled. "So when will the sale be complete?"

"Money and keys changed hands this morning."

George had approached the previous owner, a Mrs Stafford, and offered way over the odds for the business, making it clear he wanted to buy it whether she wanted to sell or not, the same as he'd done with Lil and the laundrette. Stafford had taken a little persuading—she'd built the business up since she was twenty, it was precious to her, and although she was fifty now, she felt she still had a lot of cutting life left in her.

"Then use that life for something else. Spend the extra money we give you on travelling, seeing a bit of the world instead of chopping hair day in, day out."

It had clearly appealed, because she'd agreed.

Who wouldn't agree when offered fifty grand to play with?

As with Under the Dryer, the other salon they owned, certain things would be stored here behind a fake wall in a room safe. Stacey was aware it would be there but not what it was, and if the police ever came to do a raid, she'd have to claim innocence.

He and Greg ensured they planned everything meticulously so they wouldn't get caught doing anything nefarious, although their name had been put forward by the pathologist, Jim, that they could be the vigilantes running round delivering the bodies Janine just so happened to be searching for.

Leaving notes with the dead for the police to find would stop now. It would be as if the vigilante had disappeared, and any corpses that needed to be discovered instead of chopped up and dumped in the Thames would appear as regular murders.

George handed Stacey a set of keys. "Right, all yours. All staff bar you will be freelance, they can pay their own tax and whatever, less hassle for you and us. Let me know when you've found enough stylists and we'll do a grand opening."

Tears filled Stacey's eyes. "Thanks for this. I was going batty at home, bored out of my mind. Chaz is happy to take care of me, but there's only so much yoga you can do to pass the time."

George smiled and gestured to Greg for them to leave. Out on the pavement, he scanned the street. A Chinese takeaway next door, a newsagent beside that, and then a Tesco Express, the sum of shops on the small housing estate. People around here were a good bunch, rough and ready but genuine types who rarely gave them any gyp. Those who liked their acrylic nails would be pleased because George had ordered all the gubbins for Stacey to have two nail technicians at the salon, and Stacey would stay there today to wait for it to arrive—new stations, chairs, and shelves to store the polishes.

An old woman trotted out of Tesco, her cane stabbing the pavement. She spotted them, changing direction to come and see them. "What the fuck are you two doing here?"

George would never get over those who remembered them as kids and still saw them as such. They didn't hold back and rarely had much respect, not like those who were shit-scared of them. Sometimes, George let it slide, like he did with Lil.

"All right, Mrs Robbins."

"I was until I saw you. It can only mean trouble when you're around. I doubt you've changed much since you were kids. Little fuckers."

"I don't beat people up in the street anymore." He smiled. "Not unless it's dark."

"Like I said, fuckers, and you'll have men to do the beatings for you, I'll be bound. So what's going on for you to be here? Anything I need to worry about?"

"Nah, we've just bought the salon."

"She said she was selling but not who to. I should have known it'd be you pair. I'm that pissed off because she let the staff go—was that on your say-so?"

Greg snorted and walked away to peer at the Chinese menu in the window.

"Yes, and they've been given redundancy money. Our manager will be taking on her own people."

"Well, have her get hold of Jessie, get her back. She's the one who does my barnet. I don't like anyone else, and if she's not there, you won't be getting my custom."

"What, even if we give you seventy-five percent off?"

Mrs Robbins' eyebrows shot up. "Well, since you're being so kind, I suppose I *could* try someone else…" She eyed him. "Or is it one of those senior citizen discounts? I don't want you feeling sorry for me because I've got grey hair and a dodgy hip."

"No, call it an apology for when we ran around with those plums."

She narrowed her eyes. "I bloody *knew* it was you because you were caught plumming Mrs

Vale's house later that day, too. You also broke her window if I recall."

"Yeah, well, she upset our mum."

"Ah, God love her. She brought you up well enough to defend her, I'll give her that much."

George bristled. Was she having a pop at their precious mother? "But not well enough for other reasons?"

Mrs Robbins flapped a hand. "You took it the wrong way, so don't get aerated with me, young man. Your mum was a diamond. She had to be to put up with you two for a start. Anyway, I'm off. Don't forget my discount." She ambled away.

George popped his head in the salon to let Stacey know the old girl was on permanent cheap haircuts. "Oh, and one more stipulation. You become our ears in here. Anything iffy going on, you let us know."

"Will do."

George joined Greg outside. "You feeding me oats for breakfast like I'm a fucking horse isn't cutting it. I'm starving. We'll nip to the Noodle."

Greg had changed his diet, going for healthier options, and tried to foist it onto George, who wasn't happy about it. In the BMW, Greg drove and George took a lemon sherbet from the glove box to stop his stomach complaining.

"What's on the agenda this week?" Greg asked.

"Dunno. Maybe a tour of all our businesses, show our faces on the Estate while it's quiet. It won't hurt for people to see us out and about."

"We need to find the parents of that bloke who got killed in the house fire last night once we know whether it was arson or not."

"And whether he earned being burned to death."

"Hmm, but if someone's going round meting out justice, we ought to keep our ears to the ground so we can find out who it is."

George didn't like the idea of someone enacting revenge on…what was his name? Pax Shaw. Mason, their private detective, was poking into who Pax was to see if there was anything in his past that would let them know if he deserved what he'd received.

"Maybe we ought to get Flint to check Pax out an' all," George said. "A little job to get him bedded in. Nice and simple."

"Yeah, not a bad shout."

George sent the copper a message and popped their work burner in the cup holder, ignoring the bleep of Flint probably sending one back. "I'm not sure Janine chose the best man for the job when she picked Flint."

"No, me neither, but maybe the county line runners fucked off when they realised Joe was 'missing'. They might think he's been picked off by some other county line. Flint sounded like he was telling the truth when he said he was watching them undercover, so it could be a coincidence."

"Yeah." George picked the phone up again.

GG: ANY WAY YOU CAN FIND OUT WHETHER F WAS BEING HONEST ABOUT THAT UNDERCOVER JOB?

JANINE: NOT IF IT'S A CLOSED OPERATION. HE SAID THAT WAS THE CASE. IF I START ASKING AROUND, IT'S GOING TO BE OBVIOUS SOMEONE ON THAT TEAM HAS LEAKED WHAT THEY WERE DOING. WE COULD DO WITHOUT THE QUESTIONS AS HE MIGHT THEN BE WATCHED.

GG: HOW HAS HE BEEN WHILE YOU'VE TAUGHT HIM THE ROPES?

JANINE: SURPRISINGLY ALL RIGHT. I'VE HAD HIM REPEATING THE LESSONS TO ME SO I CAN SEE IF THEY ACTUALLY WENT INTO HIS HEAD. GIVE HIM ANOTHER

FEW DAYS, AND I CAN STEP DOWN FOR THE MOST PART, ALTHOUGH I'LL REMAIN ON HAND RIGHT UP UNTIL I GO ON MATERNITY LEAVE.

GG: RIGHT, THANKS, BUT ONLY LIGHT DUTIES. I DON'T WANT YOU AND THE NIPPER IN DANGER, REMEMBER.

JANINE: THAT'S WHAT I MEANT. I'M NOT ABOUT TO GO GALLIVANTING AROUND WITH A BUN IN THE OVEN. GOT TO GO.

George sighed. "No can do on Janine finding out whether a team was in place regarding the line."

"There's bound to be one." Greg swung into the car park behind the pub. "I expect runners fuck off all the time, saves them being too predictable and easy to catch. They'll have set up camp elsewhere."

George had put one of their men on surveillance in a vehicle on Kitchen Street where the drug trap house was located in one of the boarded-up properties. So far, no comings and goings, and the police hadn't been there either. That was the bit bugging George. Flint had said his team was aware it existed, so why hadn't it been raided?

The other day, Janine had passed on that Joe was in the frame for killing his father, Pete. A gun had been found at his flat, although the bullet striations didn't match those of the gun used to murder Pete. She'd steered the investigation towards Joe being the guilty party easily, as he happened to go missing the day of the murder.

"We'll keep it in mind that Flint could be involved," George said. "In the meantime, we'll still use him."

Greg shut the engine off. "But if we find out he's the one who tipped the runners off, then he's fucking finished. No second chances."

"Fine by me."

They got out and entered the pub via the back door used by customers when they wanted a smoke in the beer garden. A quick veer right, and they were at a door marked PRIVATE, Nessa Feathers' office. George knocked, and with no response, he led the way into the bar. As usual, he puffed up with pride at how busy it was, all the tables filled with diners. Cut-price food was the draw, and the smell of several full English breakfasts reminded his stomach to growl.

Nessa worked behind the bar with two other staff members and stopped bottling up once she spotted them. She came over and smiled. "Breakfast?"

"Not for me," Greg said, "but this greedy bastard wants something."

"Oi, less of the greedy." George elbowed him. "He's feeding me oats, Nessa. *Oats*."

She laughed. "Do you want the works?"

"Please, and two coffees."

She put the sale through so it transferred to the kitchen but closed the till drawer after it had popped open. The twins didn't pay for food in here, the business did. Nessa walked over to the cups on the back of the bar and collected two. She handed them over. "Unless you want me to come round the front and do it for you?"

George had recently ordered a self-serve machine, a right old beast that did teas and hot chocolate as well as coffee, which sat at the end of the bar. Refills were free, and unless some cheeky fucker took the piss and sat in here all day guzzling, they were welcome to help themselves once they'd paid for the first one.

"Nah, I'll do it." He glanced around. "Everything been all right?"

"Yep, although I think a blast from the past is in. I can't be sure, because I must have been a teenager when I last saw him, but I'm sure that man over there in the navy suit is The Guv'nor."

George didn't look that way, not yet. "Fuck me, I haven't seen him for years."

Nessa raised her eyebrows. "My dad thought Ron had banished him."

Dickie Feathers had worked for Ron as a heavy but was now dead.

"Maybe he did," Greg said, "and he's since found out Ron's snuffed it."

"Wonder what he's doing back?" George mused.

"We'll go and find out." Greg led the way.

George smiled at Nessa, knowing damn well he didn't mean what he was about to say. "Apologies in advance if there's any aggro."

Chapter Seven

A year after that special last night with Ron, Lil lay in a heap on her bedroom floor, her body aching from the vicious battering. This was the last time she'd let that bastard boyfriend of hers do this to her. Previously, he'd only hit her body, places where she could hide the bruises with clothes, but tonight he'd gone for her face, too enraged to think straight, and now Ron would know what she'd been putting up with.

He'd go fucking ape. He'd promised her this man was a diamond geezer, and because she'd wanted Ron to have faith in his ability to pick a good partner for her, she'd kept quiet after every thump, kick, or pinch. She didn't want him to know he'd failed and misread the fucker's personality. After all, Ron expected loyalty, to be obeyed at all times, and his employee hadn't done that. "You touch Lil, and I'll kill you," hadn't registered.

Maybe it would now, because Lil wasn't going to be his punchbag anymore.

She'd been hoping for someone who'd make her feel like Ron had, but those emotions were always just out of reach—Ron was still on a pedestal, he'd been so good to her, and no one could top that. Because she wouldn't let them. Couldn't allow herself to fall in love with anyone else.

She went to the cottage every now and then, using the car Ron had bought for her as yet another parting gift, a nifty red Mini with a soft-top, caramel-coloured roof. He'd only ever arrived once while she was there, looking at her with pain in his eyes, like he wanted to touch her but couldn't trust himself. He'd opened the steel room, so she'd followed, standing against the doorjamb to watch him. He'd gone down through the trapdoor—there must be a ladder—and came back ten minutes later, sweaty, his clothes a bit grubby.

"Had to make room," he'd said, "so I moved them all under the kitchen."

She supposed the crawl space spanned the whole cottage, and any amount of bodies could be left there, no one any the wiser. Oddly, it didn't bother her, those corpses, and whenever she came here to get a couple of days' break, there was never any of that nasty smell. Maybe the steel room stopped it from infiltrating the rest of the cottage.

"I'm going to be busy for an hour or two." He'd smiled.

She'd nodded. "I'll make myself scarce. Go home."

"No need, this room's soundproof."

He'd brushed past her, his chest touching hers, and he'd given in and fucked her there, the jamb digging into her back. Then he'd walked out, returning with a man who had a black sack over his head.

"The little cunt's into kids," he'd said by way of explanation, then dragged him into the steel box and shut the door.

She sighed, wishing he'd never set her up with Jake the Rake, wishing she could have chosen someone herself. Jake was one of Ron's men, all brawn and height, just the sort she usually went after, someone with a bit of menace about him. Except she hadn't thought he'd turn that menace on her. Hadn't thought he'd dare.

Tonight, the last straw had come because of how he'd spoken to Mum. She sat downstairs in the kitchen at the minute, oblivious to what Lil had just been through in the bedroom. Lil was adept at keeping any screams or noises of pain inside her, Jake threatening to kill her if she so much as squeaked. He knew Mum didn't hold with all that bully malarkey, not a man against his woman anyway, and she'd have either been on the blower to Ron or the police as soon as she'd got an inkling something was going on.

Lil reached up to grip the edge of her bed and pull herself into a sitting position. Her ribs ached, but she didn't think he'd broken any. She'd been keeping this to herself for six months since Jake had turned cruel, hoping he'd change back to the man he used to be, the one before the fists had come flying, but she had to admit defeat now.

Not defeat, exactly, but admit that it was time.

Time to kill him.

She'd been plotting it for ages, especially in the middle of a kicking, thinking up ways to do it, taking herself away inside her head from the real-life violence to that playing out as a fantasy. She'd stab him, she'd shoot him, she'd whack him over the head with a tyre iron. She'd burn him, suffocate him, or push him in front of a train. First, though, she'd torture him in the steel room, him hanging from the chains.

She'd done what Ron had told her, fuelling the fire.

Jake had left ten minutes ago, calling a cheery goodbye to Mum as though he hadn't just beaten her daughter up. Mum had thought Jake was a keeper until tonight, when she'd voiced her opinion on how he seemed to control everything Lil did, even down to the hours she kept in the laundrette and the late nights when she was out singing with Ron.

"Mind your own business, you nosy fucking cow," he'd said.

And that had been it for Lil. The hurt on Mum's face, the shock, had prompted Lil to push him in the chest.

"Don't you ever *talk to my mum like that again. Get the fuck out!" She'd stormed into the hallway and opened the front door, waiting for him to leave. Naïve of her, to think he'd do what she'd asked because Ron had her back.*

He'd walked up to her, gripped her hair, and whispered, "Upstairs, whore."

She shrugged off the memory and washed her painful face, the water turning pink from blood. Her top lip was so sore, puffy and split where his knuckle had jammed it against her teeth. She returned to the bedroom and found her phone, sending Ron a message.

LIL: CAN YOU MEET ME AT THE COTTAGE? AND BRING JAKE?

RC: YOU'D BETTER NOT BE SAYING WHAT I THINK YOU ARE.

LIL: HE NEEDS TO GO IN THE ROOM.

RC: JESUS FUCKING WEPT! GO THERE, NOW!

She walked downstairs, dreading showing Mum her face. She entered the living room, tears welling, blurring her vision.

Mum gawped. "Oh my fucking good God, love! Did he *do that?"*

Lil nodded. "It's not like I'd have done it to myself, is it?" She laughed, and the tears dislodged. She could see Mum clearly now. Her expression… Lil never wanted to see it like that again. "It's all right, Mum. I've told Ron. I have to go and meet him."

"How long has it been going on?" Mum got up off her chair, wincing. She'd been doing that a lot lately, as if her bones were seizing up.

"This is the first time it's been my face, put it that way."

Mum drew her in for a hug, mindful to be gentle. "You said you told Ron. You know what that means, don't you."

Lil pulled back. "Best we don't talk about it, eh? If we never said it out loud, it didn't happen."

Mum nodded. "Ron's going to be steaming. He *picked that fucker for you. I've a good mind to have a word with him myself. Ron, I mean. He isn't exactly a great judge of character, is he." She paused, holding the tops of Lil's arms. "But what Ron says goes, eh?"*

"Hmm. I'd best get a move on."

"Be careful. Don't get caught up in…in what we won't speak about. Let Ron deal with it."

"I won't. I'll just watch." She wouldn't.

"You deserve better."

"I know."

Lil left the room, slipping her shoes on at the bottom of the stairs. She grabbed her handbag off the hook rack on the wall and checked her keys were in there. And the other thing she'd need.

She called over her shoulder, "Lock up behind me. I doubt I'll be back tonight."

Lil put her sunglasses on and got in her car, catching a glimpse of her face in the rearview mirror. God, what a fucking state her mouth was. She messaged the women she employed at the laundrette to ask them to work it out between them as to who would do days in her place for the rest of the week.

LIL: I'M NOT WELL AND WILL PAY YOU A BONUS FOR HELPING ME OUT.

That sorted, she drove away, turning her head to the left to hide her wrecked lips when Mrs Snotty Knickers from opposite came out of her house and stared through the driver's-side window.

"Bloody nosy cow," Lil muttered.

Every shift of gears and turn of the wheel brought fresh pain. Ten minutes later, she parked round the back of the cottage, not wanting Jake to know she was there until either she was ready to see him or Ron said she could reveal herself. This would be up to him, how this went down. In the kitchen, she took off her sunglasses. Shut the door and sat at the table. She opened her bag, lifting out her homemade weapon, one she'd taken to carrying since Jake had shown her his dark side. One night, she'd glued a razor blade to a pencil, the only thing she'd had to hand that Mum wouldn't notice had gone missing. Near the base of the blade, she'd wound electrical tape, creating a pretty decent shiv.

She'd get to use it on him this evening. She'd imagined it enough, like Ron had told her to do, but it was a given he hadn't expected it to be Jake who starred in her murderous thoughts.

The sound of the front door opening and Ron's laughter had Lil shooting to her feet. She held the weapon down by her side, her hand trembling, and stood with her back to the door.

"Just wait there a sec," Ron said.

Footsteps, where he must be checking the other rooms bar the steel one. She guessed he wouldn't want Jake to see that yet. Then the creak of the hinge where he'd pushed open the kitchen door, the soft snick of it closing.

"Turn around, Treacle," he whispered.

She wanted to tell him she wasn't a Treacle anymore, but that would be silly. Pointless. So she turned, and his sharp intake of breath and the fury in his eyes brought on more tears.

"Fucking cunt," he said, low. "That fucking bastard cunt."

He took a deep breath, and they stared at each other across the room. She sensed he wanted to come over to her, to inspect her face and hold her close, but he didn't want to hurt her. He was so angry, any hug from him would be painful.

He ran a hand over his head. "I'll take him to the room. Give me ten minutes."

He left, and she dropped to the chair by the little table, the one where they'd eaten that steak dinner and she'd necked the red wine. On one hand it seemed so long ago, but on the other the memories were still as bright as if they'd happened yesterday. It was the chasm of time between then and now that stretched, months without Ron, and she worried that one day her recall would fade.

She may have waited more than ten minutes, she hadn't checked the clock on the wall when Ron had walked out, but he'd likely put any lateness down to her composing herself before she joined him. She took the razor-pencil and, keeping it behind her, made her way to the steel room. A quick knock on the door, and Ron opened it.

He nipped out into the hallway. "I had to shoot him in the foot to incapacitate him enough to wrestle him to the floor. Smacked him about a bit to subdue him. He's a big motherfucker."

"I know."

Ron winced at his crassness. "Shit, I'm so angry this happened. I thought he was a good bloke, and he promised me he'd look after you. What the fuck went on, because he's not telling me anything?"

"For six months he was fine, but since then…"

"Why didn't you tell me before now?"

"I didn't want you to feel bad."

"I feel worse because you kept it quiet, you daft bitch."

He still loves me. *"He hasn't hit my face until tonight."*

"Clearly not, else I'd have seen it. What set him off this time?"

"He was rude to my mum, so I shoved him. Told him to get out. I won't have anyone disrespecting her, Ron. She struggled to bring me up, has always been there for me. She deserves to be treated right."

"I'm hardly the best person to talk to about treating women right, but I get what you're saying. Do you want to talk to him?"

"Not really, but I want to kill him." She lifted her razor-pencil.

He laughed, but not as unkindly as he could have. "It's original, I'll give you that. A pencil is…different."

"It was all I had at the time. I needed something in case he went too far and I snapped."

He kissed her forehead. "No one is to know about this, got it? As far as anyone's concerned, he's fucked off somewhere without a word."

She nodded. "Are you going to let me in, then?"

Jake hung limply. Lil had entered what she reckoned was one of those fugue states she'd read about. Everything had gone all weird—her hearing, her sight, her emotions. It had felt the same as being underwater, sounds muffled, her strikes of the razor against his hard flesh like those in her dreams, ineffectual, where she hacked and hacked but it didn't feel as if she'd even touched him.

The blood and cuts said differently.

Claret dripped from them, slower now his heart had stopped beating, down to his feet and into the hole created by the open trapdoor. Jake hadn't spoken at all prior to his death, even when Ron had asked questions with his hand clamped on Jake's bollocks, giving them a twist.

Jake had no remorse, wasn't even scared of dying, going by how he'd stared impassively, and when she'd gone up to him, as close as she could, and she'd reached up to swipe the razor across his throat, he hadn't reacted except giving what she'd bet was an involuntary grunt.

The blood then had been a torrent, and she'd swiped him again, going deeper, the blade meeting resistance as it coasted over his Adam's apple. She'd slashed every bit of him, going behind to mangle his arse, the backs of his legs. The skin on his back had peeled apart, each slice resembling smiles. Ron had egged her on, leaning against the wall, arms folded, and even in her underwater state, she'd registered his pride.

Now, she'd finally got her breathing under control.

"Stubborn wanker." Ron came to stand beside her and studied the blood, too. "That'll stop dripping soon."

Jake resembled something from a horror film, a human colander covered in a scarlet sheen. The steel walls, floor, and ceiling were spattered with dots, as were Lil and Ron. The room stank of filthy copper pennies, cloying, the scent thick enough to touch. That was a tad fanciful, but it really seemed that way.

"Do you want to try again?" Ron asked. "With someone else?"

She chuffed out a laugh. "I think I need a break from men, don't you?"

"No, if you've got someone else, you won't think about me."

Coming from anyone else that would have sounded conceited, but there was no point in them lying to one another about it. They wanted to be together but couldn't.

"It didn't work with Jake," she said.

"Doesn't work for me either." Ron sighed. "In another world..."

"I know."

"Go and get cleaned up. I'll get him down and put him under the kitchen."

She nodded, leaving him to it. He'd clean the room and any blood she'd tracked into the cottage. He'd get rid of her clothes. Good job she had some here in the wardrobe, really.

She got in the bath and stood beneath the shower spray, reliving her first kill.

Wondering if it would be her last.

Chapter Eight

Guv didn't need anyone to tell him who these two brick shithouses were. They hadn't changed much except to grow into their adult faces and bodies, filling them out something chronic. George still had that mad gleam in his eye, a look that spoke of him being unhinged and barely keeping his temper at bay. Their grey suits, white shirts, and red ties were as identical as their features. Was this a uniform of sorts? See the red ties, know instantly who they were?

What had happened to them in the intervening years? Halibut hadn't said an awful lot, just that George and Greg had started working for Ron as teens, climbing the ranks to become the boss' favourites. Maybe that was the only reason they'd taken over the Estate. Ron must have handed it to them on a plate. George had given people Chesire smiles and kneecapped the hell out of them, his savagery knowing no bounds; personally, Guv reckoned the bloke had something wrong up top. Halibut said they'd driven around in a battered old van, then acquired a BMW, and people were shit-scared of them. Guv could see why. If they'd been this size ever since they'd become men, even he'd leg it once he got the gist they were after him.

He hadn't even spoken to Nessa about contacting them yet, so them being here was a coincidence, or maybe not, seeing as they owned the gaff. Unless Nessa had recognised him and let them know he was here. Guv had a distinctive voice, unfortunately—maybe he should have put on his Mancunian accent. She'd been a teenager the last time he'd seen her. He'd sometimes worked alongside her father, Dickie, if the jobs needed more than one man, plus they'd all gathered in The Eagle, little Nessa sometimes popping in for a Coke and a packet of crisps, Dickie telling her to fuck off because she was a sponging pain up the arse. It was bloody odd to see her in her forties, Guv missing the majority of her life.

Time had flown.

What was Dickie up to these days? And the old gang? He should have asked Nessa but hadn't wanted to draw attention to himself just yet.

Guv sipped his coffee. George used the machine to pour two cups, acting as if he hadn't seen him. Then Greg turned his way, bold as arseholes, eyeing him up, nodding to himself. Seemed Guv had been clocked, then. It didn't matter. The cover story would solve any issues. Loads of people started again when their life wasn't as exciting as they'd hoped.

The twins strolled over, and George gave Guv one of his creepy stares from the old days. Like it always had, that stare went right through him, and a shiver wound up and down his spine, goosebumps breaking out on his arms and scalp.

It wasn't from fear, just…Guv couldn't explain it. Maybe like George had a real-life devil inside him? He wasn't right in the fucking head, he knew that much.

They sat at his table, blocking the view ahead. The width of them, all muscle, and their presence was enough to let Guv know he couldn't fuck these two about and would be a fool to try. Ron had an aura, but it was nothing on this pair. Christ, they were magnetic. Whoever got it into their heads to cross them had a death wish.

"All right, Guv'nor?" George placed his coffee on the table. "Long time no see."

"Morning. I'm surprised you remember me."

"I remember most things, most people. What are you doing back?"

Guv shrugged. "It was time to come home."

George hadn't even blinked yet. "Because?"

"Do I need a reason?" That had popped out before Guv had time to engage his brain. "Sorry, that sounded rude. Didn't mean for it to come out like that."

"Yeah, it was rude. But back to your question. It depends why you left in the first place as to whether you need a reason to be here. Why *did* you leave?"

"I needed a new scene."

"So you weren't banished, then?"

Was that the story Ron put about? Lil mention it, too. "Nope."

"Interesting. What have you been up to?"

Guv wanted to say George was a nosy bark and should mind his own business, but that wasn't the way it worked with leaders. If you were asked a question, you answered it. Whether the reply was the truth or not was a different matter. "Busy having kids, a life."

"Where's that?"

"Manchester."

"Nice place. We've got a friend up there. A bloke who runs the biggest patch. I'm sure you know who I mean."

Fuck. Don't panic. You changed your name. "I didn't get involved with anything like that. Needed a complete break from being a bully."

"Get tired of it, did you?"

"Yeah."

George still stared. "I'll *never* get tired of it. I enjoy torturing people too much. As I recall, you were seeing Lil before you left London."

"I was."

"I remember seeing you together."

This bloke's got a memory like a fucking elephant. "I was out with her last night as it happens. Had a catch-up. She's looking well."

"She's a good bird. We wouldn't want her getting upset."

Guv heard what George hadn't said loud and clear. "I've got no intention of upsetting her." Time to change the subject. "I wanted to speak to you two, actually."

"Why's that, then? Are you setting up a business that needs protection?"

"No, I need a job."

George laughed, but it wasn't the pleasant kind. "You're getting on a bit, mate, and you look like you've gone to seed, so a bully job wouldn't suit you—or us. What else can you offer?"

"What's up for grabs? Have you taken over all the pubs Ron owned?"

"Ah, so you've heard he's dead. No, they went to his daughter." George grimaced.

What's that all about?

George continued. "Although she gave The Eagle to Jack and Fiona. Sold it to them for a quid or something."

"Blimey, I haven't seen them for years. I'll pop round there in a bit. I'm surprised Leona let that pub go. It was special to Ron."

"We know."

"So has she had a personality transplant? Leona was such an abrupt little tart. Waspish. Thought she was better than everyone."

"We don't have anything to do with her."

Guv knew a bad topic when he heard one, so he'd better shut his cakehole before George filled it with his fist. "So…jobs?"

"We've got a few going concerns. I can't see you being a hairdresser or doing the dry-cleaning at Lil's. There's this place—barman? Or there's Jackpot Palace."

"A casino, I take it?"

"Yep, at Entertainment Plaza. That wasn't there in your day. Get yourself down the gym to beef yourself up a bit. I can have a word with our head of security, T-T, see if he'd be willing to take you on."

That wasn't how Ron had operated. If he wanted to take someone on as an employee, he bloody well did it, sod what other people thought.

Guv pushed his luck to see how far he could go. "What's it got to do with him?"

George glowered. "What's the way we do things got to do with *you*? If I say T-T needs to be consulted, then that's what happens. We prefer our staff to be happy in their working environment, and if you have one bad apple in the basket, all the others turn mouldy an' all. All the filthy maggots spill out."

Is he implying I'm a bad apple? "Sorry, it's just Ron would have—"

"We're not Ron. We're *nothing* like him."

Guv had hit a nerve.

He ploughed on. "I was going to ask, how come you kept the Estate name as Cardigan? That only happens when it's passed down from parent to child."

George clenched his fists and glanced at Greg.

"Not that it's any of *your* business," Greg took over, "but we wanted to keep the stability for the residents. We grew up with it as Cardigan, and it felt right to keep it that way, end of."

While Greg didn't creep Guv out to the extent George did, there was still something about the bloke that unnerved him. As a pair they were formidable, but he reckoned they'd be equally as menacing on their own. He had no plans for a date down a dark alley with either of them.

He held both hands up. "No offence intended. Just a casual query."

Greg smiled. "You'd be better off not asking questions. George doesn't like that. He can get a bit…lairy. A bit violent."

Guv laughed to hide his unease. "I remember you as kids. Took no prisoners even then."

"And that hasn't changed." Greg glanced up at Nessa holding a plate of full English.

George stood and took it from her. "I'll eat that in the corner there. Guv, give Greg your number. Greg, give him ours. We'll be in touch. Or not."

He picked up his coffee and walked away, Nessa by his side. He gestured for her to sit, and they dove into a quiet conversation.

"Fuck me, he's scary," Guv muttered.

Greg rose. "Best you don't forget that. Word of warning. If you've got anything in your past we'd be worried about, it's best you tell us now. If you don't and we uncover something, you won't get a job, but you *will* be kept an eye on. Someone will be looking into you before any job offer is made. Sleep easy."

He swaggered off, and Guv let out an unsteady breath. Shit. They were going to find out his real name hadn't been used in years. He'd have to explain himself if he wanted a job. Maybe he could say he'd needed to cut ties with Ron because he'd been asked to kill a nipper—surely the twins wouldn't stand for that. Ron wasn't here to dispute it, and the name change was so Guv could hide in peace.

Yeah, that'll do.

He got up and strode past the twins' table. Greg had settled with his brother and Nessa, watching him as he went by. The stare on Guv's back felt real, heavy, and he exited the Noodle with much relief. He accepted he might not be employed by the two nutters, so maybe his visit to The Eagle was a good choice. Jack might have something going. Guv had known him well, and being a barman wasn't so bad.

Chapter Nine

Jack Pleasant stared into the eyes of a man he never thought would step foot in The Eagle again. Confusion warred with what he was actually seeing. The Guv'nor in the flesh—or a fucking good doppelganger. He shook his head. He must be imagining it, because this bloke was *dead*. Ron had killed him back in the day but hadn't said why, all very mysterious. The beard had thrown Jack off at first, but eyes never changed, and despite the wrinkles around them, nah, he wasn't imagining this, he was sure he'd got it right.

"Guv'nor," he said. "It's been a while."

"All right, mate?" Guv glanced around. "This place looks exactly the same."

Two men along the bar had picked up on the tension streaming through Jack. Old Stanley and Sonny Bates who listened out for the twins. Stanley asked Jack a raised-eyebrow question: *Did you just say Guv'nor?* Jack nodded, and Stanley nudged Sonny, leaning in for a whisper. He was probably telling him who Guv was in case Sonny had been too small to remember.

"But other things have changed," Jack said. "Like you having a beard." *Like you being alive.*

Guv stroked his chin hair. "I reckon it makes me look distinguished."

"Some would say you've grown it as a disguise."

"Nah, beards are all the rage these days."

Jack couldn't dispute that. "Is your usual still a lager top?"

"Please."

Jack got on with pouring the pint. "What brings you back here, then?"

"Relationship breakup, kids have flown the nest. Time to move on, come home. I've got a flat but need a job, so if you've got one going…"

Nah, fuck off. "Where have you been?" Jack added a dash of lemonade to the glass and put it in front of Guv. "On the house."

"Cheers. I went to Manchester."

Ron lied to me. Did he banish him and make out he'd killed him? "Any reason for that?"

"Needed a change of scenery, didn't I. Beating people up for a living had worn thin. Plus Ron asked me to kill a four-year-old child. Fuck that. I wanted out. You know how Ron could be. I was out at all hours of the night giving people a pasting, on call, barely getting any sleep. I'd burned out, wasn't much cop to anyone."

Kill a child? What the fuck? "Hmm. So he just let you go, did he? That wasn't like him, and neither was wanting a little nipper offed. Once you worked for him, unless he said otherwise, you had to stay. It was a career for life."

"I must have caught him in a good mood."

"Did you hear he's dead?"

"Yeah. Had a coffee with the twins earlier."

Did he ask them for a job, too? "You need to watch them. They're worse than Ron in some respects."

"So I've heard. Fucking weird seeing them all grown up. I couldn't wrap my head around it."

"It comes to us all, age. They're decent men, two of the best."

Guv smiled. "You used to say that about Ron, but let's face it, he was a savage bastard, not much decent about him. I've got my suspicions those twins are his."

Stanley slammed his pint on the bar. "I wouldn't let those words pass your lips again if I were you."

Guv stared his way, laughing at the threat. "What are you going to do, bash me with a walking stick?" He paused. Seemed to realise who he was speaking to. "Stan? Fuck me, you're still alive?"

"Looks like it, doesn't it?" Stanley gave him the side-eye. "Watch your mouth, son. Loose lips don't only sink ships, they make sure your executioner gets hold of you."

Sonny took his phone out and got messaging.

Guv turned to Jack. Said quietly, "Sounds like there's some truth to it, going by his reaction. You don't jump to someone's defence like that for no reason. Mind you, it could be Stan who's the culprit. Dolly was always chatting to him when she was in here."

Jack planted both hands on the bar. "Seriously, don't go there. You have no clue how bad George is. If he hears you spouting bollocks, casting aspersions on his mother, you won't live to see another day."

Guv rolled his shoulders. "To be fair, I don't think Dolly's the type to go with Ron *or* Stan. I just find it odd the Estate still has the same name."

"They had their reasons, and you don't need to know what they are."

"They already told me."

Jack widened his eyes. "You fucking *asked* them?"

"Why not?"

Jack laughed wryly. "Fool."

Guv sipped his drink. "They're that bad?"

"You have no idea. My advice? Keep your head down and your mouth shut."

"But I've missed out on a lot. I just want to catch up."

This bloke, there was no telling him. "D'you know what, I'm going to let you put your big foot in it, let the twins sort you out if they catch you nagging. I've warned you, Stan's warned you, and if you ignore it, that's your lookout."

"Steady! No need to get arsey, is there?"

"Yeah, there is, but if you choose to carry on talking crap, then you can suffer the consequences." Jack had had enough, and he made to move away, but his wife, Fiona, came from out the back.

"All right, Fi?" Guv grinned at her.

Fiona's mouth dropped open. "*Guv*?"

"The very same. You've aged well."

She scowled. "Fuck off, I'm not a bottle of bloody wine. What the hell are *you* doing here?"

"Talk about feeling unwelcome. Why are people so shocked I'm in London?"

Fiona rammed her hands on her hips. "Because Ron killed you."

Guv appeared startled by that, but he quickly masked his expression. "What? No! I told him I needed a break and moved away."

"Then why did he say you were dead?" Fiona asked.

"Fuck knows. I'd say ask him, but he's six feet under. It's a mystery we'll never know the answer to."

"This doesn't make sense." Fiona shook her head. "Or was he hiding something? Saying you were dead so you could live somewhere else without hassle? What went on back then? You were here one minute, gone the next."

"I'd had enough, and that's all. Why Ron said that, I don't know. He was fucking strange sometimes. Maybe he didn't want anyone knowing I was unhappy working for him. He had his pride, wouldn't have liked people thinking he didn't run a happy ship and couldn't keep me under his wing."

"True." Fiona gave him a funny glance then shifted along the bar to serve a customer.

"The plot thickens." Guv chuckled.

Jack wanted to punch that smug smile off his face but picked up a cloth and got on with polishing some glasses instead. "Seen Lil?"

"Yep, last night."

"How was she?"

"She didn't whack me round the head with a baseball bat if that's what you mean."

"It wouldn't surprise me if she had. You up and left her without a word, poor cow. She was steaming angry for a fair old while."

"I shouldn't have done that. I regret it big time. Still, she got over me. Was nice as pie when we had a drink in the Red Lion."

Jack knew Lil all too well, and if she was nice as pie after what Guv had done, it meant she was plotting something. Jack had kept it a secret that Ron had killed Guv—well, supposedly killed him; Lil thought he'd just walked out on her.

Jack held a smile at bay, looking forward to any future fireworks between the two. Lil was a firecracker, and she'd pay Guv back for leaving her. It seemed he'd forgotten what the woman was like as he didn't seem fazed at all.

Prick.

"Did you hear about that fire?" Guv asked out of the blue.

"Yeah. His parents come in here every now and then. Nice couple."

"Reckon he set it?"

"What, he *chose* to cook himself to death? Come on, there's less painful ways of ending it."

"Maybe he'd done it as an insurance claim but couldn't get out in time."

"Maybe." Jack put the polished glasses on the shelf under the bar.

Much as he wanted to find out more regarding where Guv had been, he had to get hold of the twins. Sonny had likely already done it, considering he'd whipped his phone out, but Jack needed to make sure. Something was off here, but The Brothers would get to the bottom of it.

"Fiona, I'm off to clean some pipes."

She nodded, knowing exactly what he meant. "See you later."

Jack left the bar and went down to the cellar. Sent his concerns to George and Greg. Then he sat on a beer barrel and contemplated Ron's lie. It didn't add up. Ron wouldn't have let Guv go because he'd been a bloody decent bully, so something must have happened where Guv needed to fuck off and Ron had spread it around that he'd killed him to cover for whatever had occurred. Or had he let Guv go because Guv had threatened to tell everyone Ron wanted a kiddie killed? Guv's explanation had sounded plausible, he could have burned out, but people were good at bullshitting, making you believe their version of events.

Like Ron.

So who was the liar, Ron or Guv? And what the fuck had gone on all those years ago for a man to want to disappear—and a leader had let him?

Chapter Ten

The second man Ron chose for Lil had gone the same way as Jake—getting himself killed. She'd just emerged from that weird fugue state, her clothes a mess of scarlet splodges, her hair splashed with it, her face. And the smell…too much copper again. A mop and bucket stood in the corner, steam curling, the scent of bleach obliterated by that metallic tinge. Ron must have gone to fill the bucket without her noticing. It scared her a bit, that she became so consumed while killing she had no idea what else was going on. There must be something wrong with her. Normal people didn't lose their sense of grounding.

Nasty thoughts entered Lil's head, and she wasn't chuffed about it. She'd asked herself the same questions before the kill, only she'd been too hyped up about what was to come to entertain them. Now they'd returned, insistent, and she knew herself well enough to know she had to address them. Make sense of them. It would drive her mad otherwise. The thing was, addressing them meant facing things she didn't want to. But she was a practical woman, and wasn't facing them better than living in cloud-cuckoo-land? Wasn't seeing Ron for who he was, despite his kindness towards her, better than deluding herself?

Was Ron picking shitbags for her on purpose? Was it some warped way of saying he couldn't—or wouldn't—have her but he didn't want her to be happy with anyone else? Even if it meant she got clouted, or in this case, spoken to like dirt? Was his remorse at picking the wrong man—both times—fake? Or worse, was he using Lil as a cover, them abusing her an excuse to get rid of the men for other reasons? With Ron, you never knew, because his mind was fucked-up and worked differently to everyone else's.

That last suspicion hurt. Being used, played with, was something she'd signed up for when she'd become a Treacle, but he'd moved the goalposts by saying he loved her (in a roundabout way). He'd made her think she was special when she might not be, and that changed things, didn't it?

She wasn't going to trust his choice of man again. If he foisted another bloke on her, she'd go on dates but nothing more. No sex, no taking him home to meet Mum.

Bodkin, named because he'd used an old-fashioned dagger when killing, hung in the steel room. Decorated with cuts and minus his meat and two veg, he was an unholy red mess. She'd gone further with this one, slicing off anything that protruded. His ears and the end of his nose sat in his mouth with his lips—why she'd done that, she had no idea and wasn't inclined to delve into the reason. The underwater rage had taken over her again, Ron's encouragement dull in the background, her own devil louder and sharper inside her head.

What she would *delve into, though, was why she was so incensed whenever anyone chatted shit about Mum. When women did it, she kind of accepted it more—being a female herself, Lil was well aware that some of them were bitches, they couldn't help themselves when it came to being spiteful. But when* men *did it, her need to fight Mum's corner went so deep it burned in the pit of her stomach. Had her mind blocked out memories from her childhood? Had she seen something that had prompted this fierce desire to protect her mother? Maybe Lil was fucked-up because her father had abandoned Mum at the drop of a hat.*

Fucking hell, I've got Daddy issues. Great.

Was that why she'd gone with Ron? Because he was much older than her and she needed that older influence?

I don't want to go there.

"I should never have gone with him," she said to Ron. "For a start, he's married."

People gossiped, and Lil had always worried Bodkin's wife, Noelle, would find out her husband was cheating, coming round to Lil's to quite rightfully rip her a new arsehole. They had a newborn baby, Hailey, and Lil should have stopped seeing him the minute she'd found out about the pregnancy, but she hadn't. What kind of woman did that make her?

Seeing Noelle in town or out and about had been a bind, guilt stacking up, and when Lil had told Ron she couldn't keep doing this, he'd said he had everything in hand. Bod was supposedly going to leave his wife, then he could set up home with Lil. She'd have been known as a homewrecker.

"It's not working, is it," she stated to take her mind off hideous things.

"What isn't?"

"Your idea of the sort of man I need is way off the mark."

Ron shook his head as if he couldn't understand how this had happened. He was a good actor, but maybe he was being genuine at the minute. "I could have sworn Bod was the right man for you. Apart from me, that is."

She rolled her eyes at that. Ron reminded her at every opportunity that he was the man she should be with but couldn't have, as though he liked sticking the knife in. He wasn't right in the head, she'd known that before, but these mind games proved it all the more. "He didn't wallop me, granted, but sometimes words hit harder than punches."

Would he pick up on what she'd really meant? Ron's words hurt. He was just as bad as Bod in that respect, but she doubted he'd ever admit it.

He sniffed. Dismissing the need to address what she'd said? "At least you told me sooner this time."

"Yeah, well, I know my worth now, and I realised that your fuck-up isn't my problem. I shouldn't keep it to myself to spare your feelings."

"Most women wouldn't dare say that shit to me," he rumbled.

Was his tone meant to scare her? Fuck that. Whether he loved her or not, he'd kill her if she crossed the line, but she found she didn't give a shit. No man, however big he was, or thought he was, had the right to treat her badly.

"I'm not most women," she said.

"I know. That's why you got under my skin."

She sighed, so tired of his reminders, words that sent her right back to the night he'd ended it with her. It was obvious he wanted her to keep revisiting it, so he was prominent in her mind, like some cock of the walk she couldn't live without. Well, she had news for him. She could live without him, and she would. And she'd have a good go at showing him that, too. "Don't start that again. It's over. Us two getting together every now and again…I cheated on Jake and Bod with you, for what, a two-minute shag against a pub wall? It's not right, even if they were arseholes. This hold you've got over me, the one you keep engineering, it has to stop."

"What about your hold over me?"

Bloody Nora. There he went again, laying the blame at her door. She was sick of his mind games. He played them in The Eagle to the point she'd contemplated not going there anymore, finding another local boozer as her home from home. Maybe the Red Lion in town, one of the only pubs Ron didn't own around here.

She faced him. "It's up to us to make it go away. We should limit the amount of times we see each other, if we even see each other at all. I'll stop coming here and going to The Eagle. You don't nip into the laundrette or even drive past. It's doable. If a magnet and a piece of metal aren't near each other, they can't be drawn together. That pull won't be there."

"Which one of us is the magnet?"

"Fuck off, Ron. That's not important."

He went quiet for a while, then mumbled, "Not seeing you will do my nut in."

"Only because you won't have control over me, and it'll only last for a while. What was it you told me? If we get involved with other people, it'll stop us wanting each other. Something like that anyway. Except I don't want anyone else, especially you. Men are trouble, and I've had enough."

"You don't get a say in this, Lil."

She turned to him, this big bad gangster, and while he stared at her menacingly, courage took hold of her.

Underneath that tough façade he was just a bloke, and he could do with being reminded of that. Some people, no matter how hard he tried to make it otherwise, weren't scared of him. "Listen to me, you." She poked him in the chest. "Your way of doing things isn't working—you're not always right. If you loved me, you wouldn't put me through this shit."

"I do love you."

"Then if you're not prepared to pick things up with me again, let me go—for good this time. When I'm ready, I'll find my own fella."

Everyone knew Ron didn't back down often. He had to have everything his own way. So when his expression changed, she knew she had him in the palm of her hand.

She gestured to a ruined Bod. "If you don't, this *is going to keep happening. Man after man, they're going to end up here, and there won't be enough space under the fucking floor if you add the other blokes you're bumping off on the quiet. And what is it with you prowling the streets on your own anyway? I know you said you like being reminded of who you used to be, but you're a wanted man by so many, there are endless people who want you taken out, and if you're by yourself, you're easy pickings. You're meant to have Sam stuck by your side so you don't get offed."*

"I control many people, but at the same time they control me."

She frowned. "What are you on about?"

"I'm a slave to the Estate and the people on it. I'm not my own man anymore. When I go out there by myself, I'm free."

"Right." She didn't have any other answer to that, but her assumption had been right—he was *just a bloke, with the same needs as everyone else. He craved having a say in his own life as much as he craved having a say in everyone else's. What a fucking contrary bastard. "So are we in agreement? I find my next fella? And let me be clear here, I'm not asking for permission, I just want to know if I'm doing it with your blessing."*

Why, though?

Because if he's with me on this, I'm less likely to end up dead in a ditch.

He inhaled a deep breath. "Yeah. What about the singing?"

"What about it? If you want the truth, I think you've been stringing me along all this time. You can't get me a record contract. I'm not destined for the bright lights. I'll sort my own gigs, you don't need to come."

"Fair enough."

"Fair enough? What, you're actually going to let me live my own life?"

Ron shrugged. "I'm letting you go, but I'm telling you, if the one you choose turns out like the others, you still get hold of me. We'll deal with him here."

She nodded. "I'm okay with that, but like I said, I won't be coming here anymore. I risk seeing you, and it's not good for either of us. Go and find a new Treacle. Lose yourself in her and get over me. I'll do the same."

"What, with a Treacle?" He smiled.

"No, you fucking dick."

His chuckle shouldn't have happened. Ordinarily, if someone spoke to him like that he'd have killed them. But Lil was different, she was *special. Still, it didn't mean she could push her luck.*

"I'll leave you to sort him out." She jabbed a thumb at Bod. "Don't you even want to know what he did?"

"You said he didn't hit you, so I'm guessing he disrespected your mother. You might need to talk to someone about that. Your level of punishment for someone being a bit rude to her is off the charts."

She jammed a hand on a hip. "A bit rude? He called her a dried-up old *slag."*

"She was a slag, though."

Anger surged so violently she had to stop herself from slashing his face with the razor-pencil. "Excuse me?"

"There's a lot you don't know about your mother."

"Like what? She slept with a few blokes? Why shouldn't she? Just because she had me, didn't mean she should be a nun."

"I could make you hate me if I wanted to."

"Don't change the subject."

"I haven't. If I say what I could *say, you'd never want to see me again."*

"Just tell me. It's probably for the best if I do *hate you. God knows I'm finding it hard to get you out of my head." She shouldn't have admitted that. It gave him power.*

"If you're sure…"

She glared at him. "Do it. Ruin what we have forever. It's the best thing for both of us."

Ron stared at Bod, perhaps because he couldn't look at her. What he had to say was either painful for Lil or he was about to lie. "When she was younger, after your dad, your mum was a bit of a goer. Kind of went off the rails and used sex as a prop. She got involved with a few blokes before she settled on Dickie."

"Dickie Feathers?"

"Yeah. It didn't last long. Six months, tops."

"But he's married."

"So am I, yet it didn't stop you."

"No, I mean I didn't think she was the type. She told me not to get involved with a married bloke, yet she did it." According to Ron. This could all be a load of old bollocks.

"Can't you see why? She didn't want you making the same mistake. Then there was me."

"Err, pardon?" A flush of heat swept up her neck to warm her face.

"Think about it. I'm a damn sight older than you. I could be your father."

All the blood seemed to drain right out of her body, leaving her cold. The swift change from hot to chilled brought on goosebumps. "Don't say that…"

"I'm not your old man, but she was with me for a few weeks until I got bored of her."

Trying to wrap her head around a man who'd shagged a mother and *her daughter, Lil backed away from him. "That's…"*

"So now you can hate me."

"You're lying. You made it up."

"Unless you ask her, you'll never know."

"If you made it up, then you don't care if you hurt me. You're no better than the others."

"But if it works, what does it matter?"

His slow smile churned her guts. She'd known he was an arsehole, but this? Jesus Christ, he was nothing but a sadistic cunt.

She willed tears not to fall. Couldn't let him know how much he'd wounded her. "Why would you fuck with my head like that?"

Ron stepped towards her, the mask he wore with her slipping away, replaced with the one he presented to people he despised. The shutters had come down, he was locking her out. It was what she'd asked for, so why did it hurt so much?

Because she'd wanted to take away his control and have it all for herself. She wanted to be the one in the driving seat, leaving him *devastated and hurt. She'd wanted to teach him a lesson.*

He shrugged. "You want out. You're the one who said this had to stop. I'm just making sure it does. I'm doing what you wanted."

It had a touch of gaslighting about it, and the rose-coloured glasses came all the way off. He knew what she felt about people who disrespected her mother, yet he'd just done it. Spouted lies about her, cast a shadow over her reputation and hoped to ruin Lil's relationship with her. That was sick. Hideous.

"Do it. Ruin what we have forever," he mimicked. "You asked, and I obeyed. Now fuck off out of my life."

She stumbled from the room, tears hot as they rolled down her cheeks. She grabbed her handbag from the kitchen, dropping the razor-pencil inside, resisting the need to go back into the steel room and swipe it across Ron's face. She threw herself outside and got in her car, treacherous sobs irritating the shit out of her. Vaguely aware of the blood that would transfer to the leather seat, the steering wheel, the footwell, and the pedals, which would put her firmly in the frame for Bod's murder, she decided she didn't care. She had to get away from that lying monster in the cottage, the man who'd professed to love her.

Maybe he did. Maybe this was the only way he could get her to cut him out of her heart. Was she going to ask Mum? Did she want to know whether Ron had told the truth? Or was it better to think he'd lied?

She made a decision. She was going to keep it to herself, fucked if she'd let him wreck their relationship. He'd enjoy watching it implode from the sidelines, and she wouldn't give him the satisfaction.

She parked up outside the house she'd lived in all her life and crept inside. Stuffed her bloodied clothes and shoes in the washing machine and set it on a cold cycle with salt. Had a shower, thinking of Mum in the Land of Nod, oblivious to what Lil was going through.

As the water splashed down, Lil got rational. Mum was entitled to do whatever she wanted with her life, and if that meant having sex with lots of men, that was her right. If she'd been with Ron, she'd have said so as soon as Lil had told her she was seeing him. Wouldn't she? But what if Mum was too afraid of him to have explained her involvement with him? Was letting her daughter go with the same man preferable to whatever threat Ron had laid on her?

Lil understood it all too well, how that man controlled and manipulated women. She'd gone into it with her eyes wide open, hadn't cared about any consequences, trumped-up cow that she was. She was young, reckless, like Mum may have been. Having a child didn't mean she had to stop living her life.

Lil remembered going to Nan's sometimes overnight. Never had she been left alone when Mum had gone out for a bit of fun. Lil had been cared for at all times, Mum's main priority. At no time had she felt frightened or abandoned. She'd been secure.

Lil switched the shower off and stepped out of the bath. Wrapped a towel around her hair and another around her body, securing it beneath one armpit. Allowed the hate to fester. Against Ron for being prepared to lie to her about the one thing he shouldn't have lied about. Fucking hell, if she wasn't so level-

headed, this could have destroyed her feelings about her mother.

She got into bed in the towels, fuck putting her nightie on.

Sleep came surprisingly easily. It always did when she'd come to a firm decision.

No more Ron. Ever.

Arsehole.

The reckoning had come, and Lil would be receiving the new arsehole she so richly deserved. Noelle stood at the counter in the laundrette, staring straight into Lil's eyes. The baby, in a pram, slept soundly.

"Where's my husband?"

Lil's guts rolled over—not through fear, but because she had to spew lies. She'd prefer to tell it how it was, but she wasn't allowed. Ron had set the whispers going, that Bod had fucked off with another woman, and it seemed this *woman didn't believe it.*

"How should I know?" Lil glanced at two ladies sitting in front of the washing machines, clearly listening.

"You were seeing him behind my back, weren't you?"

Lil shook her head, going with the story Ron had given her. "Err, no. I can see why you'd think that, but I was paid to say I'd been seeing Bod—"

"That isn't his name." Noelle gritted her teeth.

"It's the name I know him as, the one he uses when he does jobs for Ron."

"No, he'd never work for him. You're lying."

Ah, so Bod had kept his night-time activities from her, had he? That was probably Ron's idea, too. Bod knew a lot of people, and they trusted him, so he'd have been used as Ron's ears and eyes, filtering information back without anyone suspecting it was him.

"Sounds like he deceived you on all fronts," Lil said.

"What kind of woman are you to pretend you're having it away with someone's husband?"

"The kind who knows if she didn't, she'd get her face slashed—or worse. This is Ron we're talking about here. Would you *refuse to do what he asked?" Lil softened her tone. "Look, I'm really sorry for my part in this, but I had no choice, okay? I was forced into it. I wanted to tell you..."*

"But you didn't. Right." Noelle's shoulders slumped. "I get why you couldn't say, not outright, but you could have warned me on the quiet. I'd never have got pregnant then. I'd have left him when all the affair rumours started."

"Don't tell me you regret having that baby." Lil stared at the child. Cute little thing.

"Not now I've had her, no. But bringing her up on my own, that's not something I thought I'd be doing. Can you at least tell me who he fucked off with?"

"I honestly have no idea. He was seeing her in secret, letting people think it was me. You could ask Ron…"

Noelle scoffed. "Like he's going to tell me." Her features hardened. "You helped ruin my life, and Hailey's—how's she going to feel, growing up without a father?"

"I managed all right."

Noelle tutted. "Did you, though? That's debateable, considering what you've done."

"You've got every right to—"

"Enjoy the money you were paid, won't you, but I'm telling you this, if I see you, I'll spit in your fucking face. Come anywhere near my street, and I'll break your legs."

It was an empty threat. Noelle wasn't the type.

Lil just wanted her out of here. "Ron wouldn't like that."

Noelle paled but shouted, "See if I care! I'll never forgive you for this."

She grabbed the buggy handles and strutted out, walking past the window and giving Lil a glare. Lil sighed, disgusted with herself for what she'd done.

She'd never forgive herself either.

Chapter Eleven

Flint had easily gained access to the database regarding Pax Shaw. He'd struck up a conversation with a colleague who was working on the case, pondering what had gone on, and together they sat at Odette's desk and had a poke around using her login details. It wouldn't be so simple in the future, he was aware of that, but for now, he'd take the hand fate had given him.

An interesting snippet or two had come up: Pax had been cautioned twice for 'stalking', although the stories that went with those reports sounded more like crossed wires. He'd happened to be in the same places as the women who'd rung in about him, their claims waved away as coincidences—or the coppers dealing with it couldn't be arsed to look into it further. He was ashamed to say that was more likely, all that work going into a case, only for the CPS to throw it out through lack of evidence. Going to the shops and pubs was a given if you lived on the same housing estate, and no further action had been taken other than Pax being warned that if he took it into his head to loiter outside their homes, it would go further. One woman had taken out a restraining order.

Flint scanned the words, stopping on a particular sentence.

Pax had met them online using an app called Just Dates.

That brought Flint up short. *He* 'met' people online, too, although they were young girls, him posing as a boy on a site called London Teens. *He* could also be considered a stalker—using a laptop specifically for this, he wheedled real names, addresses, and phone numbers out of the trusting girls on private message, then went to their homes and schools, watching them. He used a different username with each target, playing at being their boyfriend so they trusted him enough to send him nude pictures eventually.

Once he had those, he uploaded them, safe from detection as he used a VPN to access the web. He sold them to pervy punters desperate for images of naked schoolgirls. He bribed the girls, threatening to hurt their parents, their siblings and friends, unless they left money in coloured envelopes in specific places, small amounts they could afford. That was the best bit for him, watching them appear at the locations and put the envelopes in bins or wherever. He got to soak in their fear, how they glanced around to see who he might be.

Maybe he should be more careful. The two women in this file had spotted Pax observing them, but then again, the girls Flint fucked about with thought he was a kid the same age as them so wouldn't take any notice of a man sitting on a nearby bench when they left the bribe money.

Still, this case had given him a sense of unease, and coupled with the fact he now worked for the twins and DI Janine Sheldon had warned him to pack in anything dodgy that George and Greg would frown upon, he was a little on edge.

"Blimey, coincidence aside that he's in the same places as the women at the same time, he sounds a right freak," Odette said.

"Hmm. Meeting them online then stalking them is a bit much, I have to say. Normal people don't do that."

Odette pointed to a patch of text. "It says here that both women ended it with him after a few dates because he turned 'weird', but it isn't specified why or how. Then he started appearing wherever they were. It's making me think he did it again after these two, only *this* woman went too far."

"What, she set fire to his house?"

"It isn't unheard of." She pointed at Pax's name. "People take revenge in all sorts of ways when they're rejected, which he was. Who knows, he could have been cast aside as a kid and it affects him as an adult. Hang on..." She did another search in a new window. "There you go.

Broken home by the looks of it. Sent into care. Fostered then adopted."

"So he could have been mixed up in the head."

"Shame, but it doesn't make what he did okay. I'll check whether anything's come through regarding the cause of the fire." Odette switched to the file concerning the current case and scrolled through the recent updates. "Nothing yet. I know his phone was burned to a crisp, but his SIM might be salvageable, and there's a request out to his provider for any information on their database."

"Have you looked into Just Dates yet?" he asked, needing as much information as he could get for the twins.

"I'll do that now. They must have a website as well as an app." Odette brought up a browser and tapped the name into Google. "Here we are." She navigated to the site and went straight to the Terms and Conditions tab.

Different to other dating sites, this one just so happened to have an open list of who had dated who with ratings beside it. 'Total transparency', apparently, to prevent any misbehaviour. Only real names could be used, ones that matched their credit card. Those who signed up agreed to have their pictures and information online, like social media.

Odette switched to the Members tab, and a page came up with the alphabet at the top. She selected S first, and a raft of pictures with names beneath came up. She scrolled to Shaw. Five men had that surname, but only one was called Pax—well, Paxton.

"There he is," Odette said. "He looks a damn sight different to the scene photos."

"I bet. Crispy versus raw."

"Below the belt, Flint…" Odette gave him an admonishing glance.

"What! Dark humour gets us through, you know that."

"Hmm. Anyway, he seems pleasant enough to look at, but a lot of people appear nice and friendly yet hide shit beneath the surface."

"They do." Flint always played the happy-chappie role at work, so that wouldn't have been a dig at him. Nevertheless, his nerves prickled.

She clicked on Pax's picture, and a new window opened. A list of the women he'd dated, plus how many stars he'd been given for each date, sat under his name which was in bold type along with his date of birth and how long he'd been signed up for. A couple of years.

"Ah, those two names match the women who reported him," Flint said. "And he's only dated three others. Five's not many in two years."

"Maybe he kept being rejected and needed time out in between. You know, his confidence took a bashing and he had to gear himself up before he dated again. All of them have given him five stars for the first few dates, then it's three and two afterwards, so it's clear what's gone on. The more he's revealed about himself over time, the more it's obvious he isn't a good fit for the women. I'll put the other three through the database and ask the boss if wants me to go and speak to them, see if he stalked them, too."

"Is your team leaning towards it being murder, then?"

"We're determining *what* it is before we proceed."

"Makes me wonder why Janine and her lot aren't on it."

"Because it might not be murder. Once it's clear it is, she'll take over."

Odette clicked on each woman's profile and took down their full names, writing them in a notebook. She put them in the database. None of them had police records, so she did some further snooping and found their addresses. The one Flint was interested in was the last person to date him. Avery Chambers, twenty-three, and he memorised where she lived. He was eager to message the twins to see if they wanted him to visit her.

"Avery might be the one who solves the puzzle," Odette said, "so if the boss says I can go and see her, I'll opt for her first."

Fuck it. I was going to do that.

He glanced at where Avery was employed—Harper's Financials. She'd likely be at work if she needed to cover her tracks, acting normally so she wasn't suspected of setting the house alight.

"Should I let you get on?" he asked.

Odette smiled. "Yeah, I need to go and talk this through with the boss."

Flint rose and gave her a nod. "Hopefully this will end up as nothing more than an unfortunate accident."

"Yes. He was found by the front door, so that suggests to me he wasn't trying to kill himself. Unless he was and he changed his mind when it got too hot. Panicked."

"Could you see any injuries that would point to him being killed before the fire started?"

"No, he was blackened, all his clothes stuck to him. The post-mortem's being done today." She picked up her notebook. "See you when I see you."

She walked away, and Flint went into the toilets. Inside a stall, he messaged the twins, his hand shaking as he was using a burner—if he got caught with it, he'd have a hard time explaining it to his seniors.

FLINT: LAST WOMAN PAX SHAW DATED WAS AVERY CHAMBERS, 23. LIVES AT 16 WARTON ROAD. PLACE OF WORK, HARPER'S FINANCIALS. THEY MET ON AN APP CALLED JUST DATES.

GG: GET ANYTHING ELSE?

FLINT: JANINE TO TAKE OVER IF MURDER. PAX IS DOWN AS A STALKER ON THE POLICE FILING SYSTEM, ALTHOUGH IT WASN'T PROVED. COLLEAGUE ASKING FOR PERMISSION TO VISIT AVERY FOR QUESTIONING.

GG: CHEERS FOR THE HEADS-UP.

FLINT: NEED ME TO GO AND SPEAK TO A?

GG: NO, WE'LL DO IT. GO ABOUT YOUR DAY.

A small part of Flint was glad he wouldn't have to get involved. He had his fake ID in the name of John Stokes he could have used, but it might seem off to Avery if he turned up straight after Odette.

He wandered to the cafeteria to waste the time he had left of his shift. He was supposed to be doing some housekeeping on his work computer, but he was due out of here at two and didn't want to get into any overtime—the files he had to sort would take too long.

He planned to spend the rest of the afternoon talking to his latest girl on London Teens. She took her phone to school and accessed their chats during lessons. A bit of a feisty little cow, but he'd enjoy taming her. Scaring her.

He whistled, pouring himself a coffee.

Chapter Twelve

George and Greg stood in Avery's house. She'd let them in without question, although she'd looked like she'd crapped her knickers upon seeing them on her doorstep. They'd driven here in the BMW, all official except for a fake plate. George had informed her that a copper might turn up while they were there, and if so, they'd wait in the garden until they'd gone if their conversation was interrupted. If asked, she was to claim she didn't know who the BMW belonged to.

George and Greg sat in the dining side of her kitchen.

"Why would a copper come?" she asked. "And why are you here? Did Louise get hold of you?"

She placed coffees—thankfully from a machine, so George was happy—on the table and went back to the worktop for her cup.

"Who's Louise?" Greg reached for his.

"My friend. She stayed over last night." Avery sat opposite them. "I took the day off because I'm bloody knackered. Didn't get much sleep."

George studied her. Puffy eyes, so she'd either been crying or had sat up all night. Guilty because she'd set fire to Pax's house? Was her 'crapping it' reaction because she was afraid they'd twigged what she'd done?

"Why's that?" George asked.

"You've heard about Pax Shaw dying, right?"

"Yep."

"He'd been round here yesterday, asking if we could try again. I met him on a dating site."

"Just Dates."

"Um, yes. How did you know?"

"We know a lot." George smiled. "Carry on."

"He was fine at first, Pax, then he went weird on me on the fourth date, guffing on about us getting married and having kids. I didn't want anything serious, otherwise I wouldn't have been on that app. I mean, the name says what it's all about, just dates. It's for people who don't want anything serious. Anyway, as he *was* getting serious, I said I didn't want to see him again and told him why. Then he started turning up where I was, the supermarket, stuff like that, then my work."

"He was a stalker, did you know that?"

"No! I wouldn't have dated him if I had. I'd have a screw loose to do that. How did you find that out?"

"You don't need to concern yourself with that. But as I said, a copper's coming here. Now, I doubt very much they think you killed him by setting that fire—"

"What?"

"Let me finish. But I do believe they'll want to speak to you about any stalking that may have occurred. Sounds like it did to me. They might also want to know why you haven't phoned in about him being here yesterday. Makes it look like you're hiding something. As you're the last woman he dated, they'll want an alibi off you. We're here to a) see if you killed him and why, and b), if it was a justified kill, we'll help you get away with it. So what's what?"

"*I* didn't do it. I didn't even know where he lived until I saw it on the news, and the only reason I know now is because his house was near the end of the row and the street sign was on camera. We got a taxi back from dates, and he always asked the driver to take me home first."

"So that's how he knew where to come yesterday."

"Yes."

"In future, get dropped off in the next street over. People are fucking weirdos sometimes, and letting them know where you live before you trust them properly is a bit daft—and potentially dangerous. Still, lesson learned. Do you know of anyone who'd want to kill him?"

"No, he was closed off when it came to talking about his life apart from his mum and dad. He spoke about them a lot, said they'd adopted him. He loved them, that much was obvious, which is why I agreed to go on a second date. He was respectful of them, the sort of man I was looking for. I know I said I didn't want anything long-term, but dating a nice bloke is a bonus." She paused. "I was worrying about something, though."

"Like what?"

"Whether Pax had a friend who knew about me not wanting to date him anymore and he'd been sent here to shit me up." She laughed. "It sounds ridiculous when I say it out loud, but in my head it makes sense."

"Why would you think that?"

"Last night, when me and Louise had gone to bed, my Alexa started playing this really creepy music. It shocked me, but I didn't think anything of it because she's come on randomly before, just not at night. So I got up and shut her up, and because I was wide awake, I came in here to make a cuppa. We'd been sitting at this table earlier in the evening—I had a tea, Louise had a glass of juice. Louise offered to wash up before bed, but I said no. So when I saw the cup and glass washed up on the draining board, and Louise said she hadn't done it, I shit myself. I checked the back doors there, and they weren't locked. I'd forgotten to do it after my cigarette—I know, I'll be more careful going forward. So someone had come in, washed up, maybe put Alexa on, then left. Nothing was taken—my laptop was still on the table. That's why I said I thought someone had been sent just to scare me. Maybe so I'd run to Pax for protection? Get him to stay here for a while? You see that manipulative shit on the telly, so it's plausible, isn't it?"

"Yep. And this happened after Pax had died."

"Yes, it had already been on the news, and that's why Louise came to stay because I felt bad."

"Why?"

"I'd told him I'd ring the police if he bothered me again, and I thought he'd gone home and killed himself in the fire. Sounds like I'm up my own arse saying he'd top himself over me, but your mind does all sorts when you're panicking. It was such a shock to hear his name on the telly."

"When did Louise arrive?"

"Five-something. I'd rung her before Pax turned up so I could tell her he'd been standing outside my work again, and she heard my conversation with him at the door. She left work and came straight here. It only took her ten minutes. Based on where he lives, I wouldn't have had time to go round his, set the fire, then get back before she arrived."

"Tell the copper that. Even if you went in a car you'd still be stretched for time. If you get any gyp off the Old Bill, let us know. We can make any pressure go away, if you catch my drift." George held out his hand for her phone. "Unlock it so I can put our number in there." He did that then placed it on the table. "So if he didn't set the fire, who the fuck did?"

"No idea." Avery sipped her coffee. "Could it have been an accident? Then again, you said he was a stalker. What if another woman did it? What if he was seeing someone at the same time as me? You're supposed to leave feedback on the dating app, rate with stars, but she might not have. All that crap about marriage and babies could have been what he did, fucking with people's heads, seeing who was in it for the long haul."

"I'm sure we'll find out one way or the other." George drank half his coffee in one go. "I'm satisfied you're not dodgy, so we'll be off. You'll want to get some CCTV put up in case your washer-upper comes back."

Greg stood. "Nice meeting you."

They left, Greg driving them round to Pax's. Two women stood on the corner, gassing. They glanced over, clocked the BMW, and their eyes widened.

Greg stopped nearby and wound the window down. "Got any news?"

One of the ladies came over. "There's a fire officer in there now. Something about discovering the seat, whatever the fuck that means. I was earwigging and caught his conversation with a copper."

"The seat of the fire—where it originated. What's the gossip?"

"That something caught fire and he got trapped. He was found by the front door, on the floor, so smoke inhalation must have got to him."

"Cheers."

George passed an envelope to Greg who held it out of the window. The woman took it, seeming proud as punch she'd received a nice little earner.

"We weren't here," Greg said and drove away. He pressed the button to raise the window and glanced at George. "So he was trying to get out."

"Hmm. The question is, was it smoke that stopped him or something else?"

"Chuff knows. We'll get more out of his parents."

"I wonder if it's the Shaws who live near The Eagle. Do you remember old Wilf? He always bought us sweets. Avery said Pax was adopted. The Shaws were foster parents."

Greg changed direction. "We'll go and find out. Jack will know."

"I wanted to go to the pub anyway, what with Guv turning up and saying shit. I really want to break his fucking kneecaps for that Ron comment."

"About him being our dad?"

"Yeah. We don't want that kind of nonsense being spouted."

"What if Guv knew the truth? He was one of Ron's most-used men as far as I can remember. He always seemed to be doing something for him."

"Yeah, the amount of spying we did on Ron as kids, we saw a lot. You're right, Guv always seemed to be at the office or out on a job. The thing is, Ron played the devoted husband, it wasn't common knowledge he had Treacles on the side."

"Probably because whoever suspected it, or knew for sure, had been threatened to keep it quiet. Or they just knew not to open their mouths. Ron wasn't someone you accused of anything unless you fancied a bullet in your head. I find it funny that he didn't know people were aware of what he was up to. He thought he was so clever, but his secret might not have been so secret after all."

"Hmm. Park there, look."

Greg tutted. "I saw the empty space myself, thanks."

"Keep your wig on, I was only helping you out."

They entered The Eagle, greeted by Jack's sour face, Stanley tucking into his free meal of the day, courtesy of Fiona, and Sonny doing the same beside him. Sonny and Jack had sent messages earlier, and both men had a feeling Guv wasn't on the level.

"Afternoon," Jack said.

George and Greg nodded greetings to the other customers and approached the bar.

"Shall we chat?" George asked, except he wasn't exactly asking but telling. He gestured to

Stanley and Sonny. "Bring your lunch. I want you two in on this an' all."

"I'll get drinks sorted," Fiona said.

Jack led the way to his back room where Ron used to hold poker games and rinse the players of their money. They all parked their arses around the table, Stanley getting right back to the business of eating. Today's special was Fiona's chilli, which, to be fair, was the special most days. She came in with a tray of bottles, three beers and two Cokes.

"Do you two want some lunch?" she asked.

"I'm all right, thanks," George said. "Still full from my second breakfast. The first was like throwing a sausage down the high street, didn't touch the sides."

Greg tutted. "Shut up, bruv, you're boring me now."

"What's gone on?" Stanley asked.

"I dared to feed him porridge for breakfast. He's just being his usual annoying self by keep bringing it up." Greg nodded to Fiona. "I wouldn't mind a bowl, ta."

Fiona retreated, the door snicking shut behind her.

"I love a bit of porridge," Stanley said.

George snorted. "Well, I don't. Not the stingy portion he gave me anyway." He leaned forward to take a Coke. "What time did Guv leave?"

Jack grabbed a beer. "Fiona said he fucked off not long after I went down to the cellar to message you."

Sonny had finished his food and pushed the bowl away. "Yeah, he drank his pint then walked out. Didn't even say goodbye."

"Did you go after him?"

"Of course I did. I wanted to see if he had a car or was using Shank's pony."

"And?"

"No motor. He went off towards the factory. Maybe he was going to ask about a job."

"He asked me for one," Jack said, "but I ignored it and talked about something else."

"He was after one off us an' all." Greg looked up.

Fiona had come back. She handed him his chilli with a side of garlic bread. "So he's desperate for an income?"

"Maybe. We've got Mason looking into him," George said. "I want to know exactly what he was up to in Manchester. What guff did he give you?"

Jack swigged some beer. "Said he left London because he needed a change of scenery, got tired of being Ron's bully. Something I think he's bullshitting about is he said Ron asked him to kill a four-year-old. Ron was a bastard, but I can't see him ordering that to be done. Guv reckons Ron just let him go, yet Ron told me he'd killed him."

"And me," Fiona said. "Although we were sworn to secrecy. Shit, I'd better get back out to the bar." She paused at the door. "If you need anything clarifying, I'll come and have a chat after Jack relieves me."

She left, and George indicated for Jack to continue.

"We chatted for a bit about you two, how you'd grown up and whatever, then he comes out with the gem that he thinks Ron was your dad."

Stanley gave George a knowing glance. The old man knew the truth of it all because he'd been there for the twins' mother, but he would keep his mouth shut on that in front of the others. "Cheeky bastard. Everyone knows your dad was Richard. I told Guv to keep his thoughts to himself in future. Said his executioner would come for him if he kept on."

Jack twirled his bottle around on the table. "He went on about it to me after that, saying there must be some truth to it if Stan had piped up."

George's anger burned. If Guv was gadding about saying shit like that to other people, it wouldn't take long for the older folks to put two and two together. That would mean George and Greg would have to spend time on damage control, something they didn't need in their busy lives.

Jack scrubbed a hand down his face. "After I warned him to shut his trap, he changed tack and said he didn't think Dolly would have gone with Ron, then banged on about the Estate having Cardigan's name."

"He had the brass balls to mention that to us." Greg loaded up his spoon with chilli. A kidney bean plopped off into the bowl. "He needs teaching a lesson."

"Maybe go and see Lil," Jack suggested. "He said he'd been out for a drink with her last night, which surprised me, to be honest. I didn't think she'd have given him the time of day, but Guv reckoned she was nice as pie, as he put it. She'll be up to something, you mark my words."

"Not a bad shout," George said. "What else was said?"

"He changed the subject and brought up the fire two streets over."

Now *that* was telling, unless Guv had picked it out of the air for something to say. It was all over the local news so not surprising that people were talking about it.

"We're poking into that ourselves," George said. "It's got a dodgy feel to it. I wonder why he's interested in it?"

Jack stopped fucking about with the bottle and folded his arms. "He was saying whether Pax set the fire himself. Fucking weird conclusion to come to. Whenever I hear about a fire, my mind goes to arson first and an electrical fault second. Guv mentioned an insurance claim."

"Do you reckon he knows something?" Greg picked up a slice of garlic bread and bit into it.

Sonny frowned. "How long's he been back? What I mean is, did he only show his face yesterday, or has he been here for a while? Maybe he got involved with Pax somehow and *Guv* set the fire. Nah, that's a bit farfetched, ignore me."

"We won't dismiss *any* theories." George looked at Jack. "Do Pax's parents still come in here?"

"Not often these days, they're getting on a bit, but yeah."

"Do you know where they live? I've got a rough idea, but I haven't seen Wilf for a while. He used to do some message-running for Ron."

Jack gave him the address. "Watch him, he's got heart issues, and this shit going on with his son…"

"Yeah, we'll tread lightly. We'll go round under the guise of wanting to help them with the funeral."

Sonny chortled. "No point in having a cremation because he's already had one."

George laughed. "You sick fucker."

"You've got to have a bit of banter, haven't you." Sonny drank more beer. "Keeps you sane."

George necked the rest of his Coke. "Right, if Guv comes back in, engage him in conversation. I want to know more about what he's been up to, why he left so suddenly—because his explanation isn't cutting it—and why he's come back. The real reason."

In the bar, George waved to Fiona and waited in the car for Greg who was finishing his lunch or maybe visiting the loo. He stewed. Guv being a ponce by talking about things he had no right to had really got on George's tits. *Had* Ron confided in Guv about his affair with Dolly? If he had, was Guv only bringing it up now because Ron wasn't here to kill him for opening his mouth? Or did Guv still see himself as a hardman, someone unafraid of the twins, so he'd say whatever the fuck he liked?

Greg came out and got in the driver's seat, his hands wet.

George needed to get some of this angst out of him, so he'd wind his brother up because it was something he could control. "You either pissed over your fingers, you dirty bastard, or you didn't use the hand dryer."

"Pissed myself? Sod right off. I don't use the dryer because I read something about faecal matter being in the air and the dryer wafts it about, makes it stick to your skin."

"Faecal matter?"

"Shit, George."

"Oh, that's nasty. Thanks for that."

Greg set off towards the Shaws' place. "What have you been thinking about? Actually, don't tell me. Guv saying about Ron being our dad."

"It's like you live inside my head."

"I'm glad I don't, it's a nightmare in there, but I know what sorts of things naff you off the most. Like I said, Guv needs teaching a lesson. I don't want him working for us if that's the type of crap he's going to be telling people. I'm not having Mum's memory tainted."

"Then we're on the same page. We find out where he lives and go for him. We'll speak to the Shaws, then Lil, and after that, Guv."

Greg pulled up outside a two-up, two-down, the curtains drawn at all the windows, probably because the Shaws were mourning. The small front garden had a patch of lawn and empty pots, mud to the brims. George knocked on the door, and a short woman opened it, peering out at them from behind large-framed glasses.

She looked the same as she had years ago but with more wrinkles and a dusting of grey at the roots of her curly hair. George would make sure she got it done nice at Under the Dryer for the funeral.

Her face fell. "Oh. It's you two. I don't need any trouble."

"Don't sound so down about it, Caroline, we're here to offer help," George said.

"You'd best come in, then, but I'm warning you, we've got coppers coming back in an hour, so you're better off making yourselves scarce before then."

She led them into a stuffy lounge, an electric wall fire on full blast, fake flames dancing behind the glass front. Wilf sat right next to it, a blue blanket over his knees. He glanced at them, then looked away as if having the twins in his house was inconsequential. George supposed it was, given the fact their son had snuffed it.

"State your business then go," Caroline said. "Wilf can't cope with all the comings and goings. He's got a dicky heart."

She reminded George of Mrs Robbins outside Curls and Tongs, no-nonsense attitude, not giving a fiddler's fuck who they were.

"The funeral. We'd like to pay for it."

Her shoulders sank, as if a weight had flown off them. "That'd be a big help, thank you. We haven't got much. Pension, you know…"

Going by their ages, the Shaws had adopted Pax later in life.

"Have you had any word as to how the fire started?" Greg asked.

"I've not long heard from the fire officer as it happens." Caroline lowered into a chair on the other side of the hearth. She winced. Bad hips? "They suspect a cigarette dropped on a rug. I told him to pack that smoking in, but he didn't listen. He was an unruly little sod, didn't like being told what to do. Never could take being told no."

George glanced at Greg who raised his eyebrows. He hadn't liked Avery telling him no either, so did her story about a friend of his going round there hold water? Had Pax contacted him on his way home from her place to set everything up?

"So they don't suspect arson or murder, then?" George asked.

"No, accidental, unless something tells them otherwise, and it doesn't surprise me one bit. He was probably pissed up. There were fragments of a bottle of booze that had exploded. He always turned to that when things didn't go his way or he couldn't cope. He was bloody hard work, and we tried, but no amount of teaching him how to behave worked. He came from a severely broken home. The crap he went through, it's no wonder he was messed up."

"Why did you adopt him if he was so much trouble?"

"*Someone* had to, and he was that bad we didn't think anyone else would. We couldn't stand the thought of sending him back into that care home. We'd worked wonders with all the others and naïvely thought we could do the same for him. But then the stalking happened, and we knew we'd failed."

"We heard about that, but it's not your fault. Don't blame yourself. Some people just can't be helped."

"Given time, we might have got through to him." The house phone rang, and Caroline let out a screech. "Oh God, what now?"

Wilf grumbled something unintelligible, and it seemed to bring Caroline out of her panic, remembering she wasn't supposed to stress him.

She picked the phone up on the table beside her and answered, "Yes?"

While the conversation went on, George crouched by Wilf. "If this is something dodgy, if Pax was killed, we'll find the bastard, all right?"

Whether Pax deserved it or not, Wilf had been good to them when they'd been kids, and even if George had to lie to this man afterwards and tell him Pax had done nothing wrong, he would.

Wilf turned his watery eyes George's way. "You're a good lad, no matter what other people say."

George patted his arm and stood.

Caroline put the phone down, and it was obvious she wanted to cry. She got up and knelt in front of her husband. "Now then, don't get yourself in a state, but it might be murder, love. Pax's legs were broken, and that's why he couldn't stand to open the door."

Wilf nodded, taking the news surprisingly well, and he stared up at George. "You know what to do, son."

George nodded. "Consider it done."

Chapter Thirteen

Lil had caught Guv's eye in the Red Lion, and she wasn't sure what to do about it. For the past few weekends he'd been watching her, his interest clear. There was nothing she could do about it either, seeing as she put herself up for inspection. She'd persuaded Dave to let her set up her gear and sing in the corner on Saturday nights, free drinks her only payment. She just wanted to perform, money didn't matter. The customers enjoyed it, everyone joining in with her once they'd had a few bevvies, and it was nice not to have Ron keeping watch, giving her advice on how to stand, what to wear.

Funny how at one time she'd craved that.

She'd realised, pretty fucking quickly, that her 'love' for him had been infatuation, some twisted kind of punishment she'd put herself through, wanting what she couldn't have, and his for her was nothing more than needing control. It didn't hurt, that knowledge. She'd learned in the past three years since the night of Bod's murder that discovering things about yourself, and others, wasn't a bad thing if it meant it helped you to grow.

She finished her first set and put on some background music while she had a drink. At the bar, she chatted to a couple of people, drinking her vodka and tonic, glancing over at Guv every so often to see whether he stared at her.

He did.

Fuck's sake.

Did she fancy him? Yes. Was he one of Ron's men? Also yes, which meant she'd steer well clear, bargepole firmly in place. For all she knew, Ron could have sent Guv to watch her because he knew damn well Lil drank in this pub now, although admittedly, he hadn't been eyeing her up until recently, and this had been his favourite boozer way before she'd made it hers. But it was obvious what was going on.

Lil ordered her second drink, a pint of lemonade this time. Guv waded through the crowd, and she steeled herself for his bullshit. And it would be bullshit, a stupid little story concocted by Ron in order to get her to fall for Guv. Guv reporting back. Both of them laughing at her. Christ, he must think she was thick as pig shit.

"I love your voice," Guv said.

"Thanks."

"You sound like you don't believe me."

"Forgive me, mate, but anyone involved with Ron Cardigan who approaches me with that look on their face"—she jabbed her finger at his—"like they want to get in my knickers, is a no-go for me. Why don't you toddle off and harass someone else."

"Fuck me, love, calm down."

She glared at him. "Don't you know it's the law not the tell a woman to calm down?"

"Is it?"

"Yeah, an unwritten one."

"Ah, written by women, and men have to guess what it is. Right, I getcha."

She smiled, despite trying not to. "Had a few birds who expected you to read their minds, have you?"

"You could say that."

"Poor you. Suck it up."

He reared back in mock horror. "Bloody hell, who hurt you?"

"Wouldn't you like to know."

He raised his eyebrows. "I would, that's why I asked."

"I can't say. I might get bumped off."

Guv frowned. "Who the fuck's threatened you? I'll kill him."

She laughed. "Oh, you're good, I'll give you that."

His pint glass stopped halfway to his lips. "What do you mean?"

She shook her head. "Doesn't matter. Now, if you'll excuse me, my break's over."

She took her lemonade into the corner and placed it on the round table there. Loaded 'I Will Survive' onto her machine and belted it out, believing every word. Other ladies joined in—everyone had a story, didn't they—and some men looked sheepish, maybe knowing they'd been the cause of a woman's upset, others proud that they'd stomped on hearts. But Guv, he appeared sad as he gazed around at all the females united in solidarity, as though he thought that if men were just a tad more careful with their words and actions, this scene would never happen. But it did, in pubs and clubs across the country, wounded hearts on sleeves and hurts exposed for all to see.

Men are arseholes.

Lil had tried not to be bitter, but her experience with them hadn't exactly given her confidence of ever finding one who'd treat her right. Dad, Ron, Jake, Bod…tossers.

She finished the song and sipped some lemonade. The smoke from people's cigarettes always dried her throat out, yet when she inhaled it from her own ciggie it was fine. Annoyed she'd been distracted by Guv enough that she'd forgotten to light up on her break, she selected another song and lost herself in her passion. She'd been born to do this but had accepted she'd never be on a proper stage, loads of fans screaming her name. She wouldn't be one of the lucky ones where a record producer happened to hear her from outside, strolling in and signing her. Now she'd had time to ponder all the ins and outs of Ron and his twisted personality, she'd bet if someone had *approached him in the past to sign her up, he'd sent them away. He'd wanted her all to himself.*

An hour later, the second set came to an end, so she finished her lemonade, having sipped it between every song, and went to the bar for another drink, except this one was vodka and tonic again. Her third stint would only be thirty minutes. She always timed it so Dave rang the bell for last orders as soon as her final note had died a death, or maybe he waited until it had.

She accepted her free drink and lit a fag, stiffening when Guv came over. For God's sake! "Why don't you just fuck off?"

He smiled. "I like your attitude. It's a draw."

"More like you've been told to bullshit me."

"Eh?"

She had to admit, he did seem confused. Maybe Ron hadn't sent him to chat her up after all. But wasn't that what she was supposed to think? She couldn't let her guard down. Couldn't let Ron win another round.

"What do you want?" she asked. "If it's to ask me out, save your breath. I'm not interested."

"Why?"

"You work for Ron."

"So? What's that got to do with anything?"

"It has a lot to do with it."

Guv shook his head. "You think he told me to come on to you? That's a bit weird."

"Believe me, it isn't."

"Has he done it before, then?" Guv thought for a moment. "Nah, you're pulling my leg. I know you

were with Jake and Bod for a bit, but surely he wouldn't have set you up with them, not when you and Ron were—"

"Shut your fucking mouth," she hissed and looked around to check no one had heard him. "Don't talk about things like that. How the hell did you *know?"*

"I watch. I see things."

"Well, if he finds out you're aware… And is it so hard to believe a man like Ron didn't set me up with them?"

"Playing matchmaker? I wouldn't have him down as that sort of bloke."

"Matchmaker is one way of putting it."

"Talking of matches, I've got a job to do tonight. Want to come along for the ride?"

"A job for Ron?"

"Yeah."

"What the fuck gave you the idea I'd want to be in on that*?"*

Guv shrugged. "Dunno actually."

"God, you're like all the others, posturing, wanting to show women you're hardmen."

"Nah, I just wanted you to see who I am."

"What, a murdering bastard? No thanks."

"But if I'm honest from the start, then we'll get along better if you know there's no secrets."

"I don't want to get along with you. You're a hired man who likes inflicting pain. You'd probably hit me and all sorts." She was baiting him, wanting to see when he'd snap, proving to her he was cruel underneath it all and this was a setup. The men Ron employed didn't like being challenged by a woman, and Guv would be no different. A few more prods, and she reckoned he'd go off on one. "My days of swooning over gangsters are long gone. I'd prefer a bloke with a normal job, and you haven't got one, so sod off."

He laughed. "Fucking hell, you're perfect."

"What?"

"You don't take any shit. I like that."

"Good for you." She'd smoked her fag too quickly so lit another. Glanced at the clock. Five more minutes, and she'd be back in the corner.

"What do you want in life?" he asked.

That was a first. No bloke had ever asked her outright before. "There isn't enough time for me to list everything."

"Then tell me in the car on the way to my next job."

"Err, how about no."

"I want to get to know you."

"That's nice. And I was being sarky then, just so you know."

He ran a finger over a towelling beer mat. "Why are you so prickly?"

"Why are you like a fly on shit, annoying and won't go away?"

"Blimey. You're a hard nut to crack. Got a tough shell."

"It's called armour, now piss off and let me enjoy the rest of my break in peace."

He walked away, and she watched him go, refusing to buy whatever he was trying to sell her. He was a wanker, just like the others, and there was no way she'd give in.

Guv could go and do one. Her fanny had shut up shop.

On her way home, the rumble of a car engine brought on a pinch of annoyance, maybe a dash of fear. Not because she was worried about being attacked on the pavement—she had her razor-pencil in her handbag, easily accessed from the little pocket in there—but because the driver might be Ron. Now she'd told Guv where to well and truly get off, Guv had likely tattled to him on the phone. Ron might have come out to put pressure on her, remind her that he could insist she start seeing Guv whether she liked it or not. He'd dish out threats, maybe even mention Mum might not be safe.

She'd had glimpses of Ron over the past three years, but she'd hardened her heart in the shower the night he'd lied to her about her mother, and seeing him only brought on anger now. He never looked her way—a form of punishment, he'd think, but he was actually doing her a favour. If she saw him right this second, she'd tell him to take a running jump.

"Want a lift?"

Guv. She stopped and stared at him. His window was down, one arm leaning on the frame, a casual pose some might think was sexy. She didn't.

"Go away."

"Aww, come on, it's not safe to be out here on your own."

The East End Stalker sprang to mind, a man she'd tried to pretend didn't exist, because she was so anti men at the moment that she rebelled against any of them dictating what she did. If she got a cab home, it meant the Stalker had scared her, and she wouldn't allow that. On the other hand, she was aware of how stupid that sounded, taking a risk just to prove…what? That she had no regard for her safety?

"Are you referring to that Peeping Tom weirdo?" she asked.

"Yep. Did you hear the latest? He killed one of the women he's been spying on."

"When?"

"Heard about it in the pub earlier. She'd been found in her house but had died a few days ago. So, that lift?"

Lil shivered. "Bloody hell, all right."

She walked round the back of the car, spotting a Polaroid camera on the rear seat on top of a jacket. It gave her a second of unease, the thought of him taking pervy pictures of women in his car perhaps, but that could be her mind going into overdrive because they'd been discussing the Stalker. She got in the passenger side, strapping herself in. Guv drove away, in the opposite direction to her street, and that was another ploy, to make her think he hadn't been told to watch where she went after she'd been to the pub.

"Where am I going?" he asked.

She shook her head. "Okay, I'll play along. Do a U-turn and go the other way."

He did that, glancing across at her. "Where to now?"

She didn't want to give him her address, not when she was sure he already knew it. She could play games, too. "I don't know, you tell me."

He stopped at the kerb, yanking the handbrake up. "Look, I don't know what you think's going on, but it isn't. No one tells me which women I can go out with. If Ron did, I'd tell him to go and fuck himself. All I do for him is jobs, dirty work. He has no say in the rest of my life."

"And what dirty work is it tonight?"

"Setting fire to a workshop. Except it isn't just a workshop. Some cunt's dealing drugs out of it without permission. Ron wants to make a point."

"Where is it?"

"Arnold Way."

"Go on then, take me there."

Guv got going again, chatting about who the drug dealer was and how he'd been warned once already to pack it in. "I'm surprised Ron gave him a second chance to be honest."

"Hmm, he's not known for that."

"What's your beef with him? I know you two dabbled with each other and he used to be your manager, but how come he stopped?"

"Because I asked him to."

"Why?"

"God, you're nosy."

"I'm curious."

"He wasn't doing what he told me he would. I mean, it's not like I'm in sold-out arenas making a packet like he promised, is it."

"True."

"Anyway, he's an arse, and I don't care if you tell him that either."

"I wouldn't do that."

Somehow, she believed him, but she kept her rose-coloured glasses firmly out of the picture, because believing meant you got hurt.

Guv pulled up in Arnold Way, parking outside a place with a flat roof. It looked similar to a Portakabin except it was a proper building.

"Wait there. I won't be long."

Guv got out and opened the boot. In the light of a streetlamp, he carried a petrol can. He popped the spout through the letterbox and poured, then took a rag out of his pocket and dropped it on the ground, dousing it in petrol. Lil held her breath as he fed the majority of the cloth through the letterbox, leaving a white triangular tongue sticking out.

He stepped back a few paces and put the can down, going back to the letterbox. Struck a match, and for a moment she envisaged his hand going up in flames, his glove catching alight, but he held the match steady. Touched it to the tongue, the flash of fire at the letterbox proving there was no going back now. Orange light lit up the mottled pane in the door, and he retreated, grabbing the can and staring at his handiwork.

In a burst of movement, she undid her safety belt and knelt on the seat, reaching into the back for the camera, hoping there was film in it. She sat, twisting her body towards where Guv stood, and checked the frame counter. Six photos left. She snapped a picture of him, the flash going off. Thank God he had his back to her otherwise he'd have seen it. The photo came out of the slot, and she wafted it around to dry it faster. Camera tossed in the back, she faced forward and held the image up. There was enough light coming from the burning building for her to see.

Anyone who knew Guv would twig this was him. The shape of his head gave it away. His silhouette against the stark brightness of the orange-and-yellow glow was creepy as fuck. But she now had insurance. If he turned nasty on her, she might not even tell Ron, just go to the police instead.

Men weren't allowed to fuck her over anymore.

Chapter Fourteen

Lil had done her afternoon singing stint at Elm House and was on her way to meet the twins. They'd sent a message, saying they needed to chat about Guv. Of *course* they'd bloody heard he was back and wanted to muscle in. She'd already made plans on how to kill the fucker at the cottage and didn't need those two poking their oars in, but she'd have to rethink things, because she wasn't as young as she used to be and might need their help. It had worked out fine for Stacey and Hailey—they'd planned to kill Joe themselves then stepped back so the twins could sort it. Was it so bad if Lil let someone else take the reins, too?

As she didn't want them at her house—it was her private sanctuary and barely anyone was welcome, thank you—she'd agreed to go to the parlour at the back of The Angel. On her walk there, dressed to the nines in another of her exuberant outfits (a zebra-print catsuit she'd only bought the other day), she trotted along on her red high heels that matched today's beehive wig and handbag. People did a double-take, as they always did, but she was past giving a fuck what anyone thought of her. She felt good, and their opinions were so far down her list of priorities it wasn't funny.

Last night, she'd sat up late and written in a notebook, one she'd burn as soon as she'd memorised each step. She'd gone with the scenario of having another drinking session with Guv tonight and then she'd take him to the cottage, saying it was her secret hideaway.

Next, she'd get him shitfaced on whisky and wait for him to pass out like he used to—he never could handle a good malt. She'd chain him up, razor him to death, and leave him hanging in the steel room, then let him drop through the trapdoor.

Maybe she *should* confess what she was up to first. She wasn't afraid of the twins, but she didn't exactly want to lose her job at the laundrette, and they could turf her out by her ear if they found out she'd killed Guv without going to them beforehand. She'd given Ron the courtesy of letting him know, so she supposed it was only right she did the same now.

"Fucking hell," she muttered, hating Cardigan rules and how they prevented her from doing whatever the hell she wanted.

She trotted down the side of the pub and knocked on the back door. It had a keypad, but she hadn't been given the number. Amaryllis answered, her smile as bright as always, and Lil gave her a hug.

"How have you been?" Amaryllis asked.

"Fine until a certain person breezed back into my life, but you don't need to hear about that. I'm sorting it."

"The twins' kind of 'sort'?"

"That would be telling. Where are they?"

"In Debbie's old room over there." Amaryllis pointed. "Do you want a cuppa?"

"No, ta, but I'll probably need a stiff drink in the bar after this." Lil went over and tapped on the door, opening it and poking her head inside.

George and Greg sat on sofas, each with a mug in hand.

She slipped inside and closed the door, sitting beside Greg. "What did you need to see me for?"

"As you know, Guv's back, and we wanted to get your take on it." George stretched his legs out.

She relaxed, seeing as he seemed so chilled out. "He walked into the laundrette yesterday. I didn't recognise him at first, not until he spoke. He asked for change so he could buy some washing power an' that. I actually went cold all over."

"Why? Rage? Because he left you?"

"No, not that." Fuck, she was going to have to tell them the full story. It had suddenly dawned on her that if she was right, this was so much bigger than what she could handle. Guv being the Stalker put a different slant on things. What if he'd been back a while and had already terrorised women? Yes, she could get him drunk, but should she take the risk? What if he didn't pass out? What if he got funny with her? What if *he* murdered *her*? No one would know because the cottage was remote. "I'm glad you messaged, because I need to speak to you about something."

"Like what?"

"I'm going to kill him, just so you know."

George sat forward. "Why?"

She launched into her story, and it sounded so silly now, that she'd suspected him of being the Stalker, but at the time it had been so real, so plausible—what she'd seen that awful night was proof enough. Once she'd finished telling her tale, she wished she'd taken Amaryllis up on her offer of a drink. Her mouth had gone bone-dry.

"Fuck me." George shook his head. "So he fucked off right when you were going to tell Ron your suspicions?"

"Yes, so naturally, I thought Ron had found out by himself because Guv just wasn't around anymore."

"He told Jack and Fiona at The Eagle that he'd killed him, swore them to secrecy."

"What?" Lil calmed down from the shock of that. "Okay, that would make sense because Ron would want to cover the fact Guv had gone without permission, but he clearly *didn't* kill him, so what the fuck went on?"

"We likely won't know unless Guv tells us, and the only way we're likely to get that out of him is if we string him up. When did you plan to kill him?"

"Tonight."

"Where?"

"Somewhere safe."

"I thought you were going to say at your house for a minute there. You don't want to shit on your own doorstep. And you haven't killed before, so things could go wrong."

He eyed her oddly, as if he didn't believe what he'd just said, and once again, Lil was convinced Ichabod had spilled her secret about Jake and Bod, although she hadn't told him about the cottage or their names. She could understand why the Irishman would have passed the news on. George had likely told him to keep his ear to the ground and report back, but she didn't like it. But maybe it was just her suspicious mind yabbering on and she was doing Ichabod a disservice.

"You don't sound too sure about that," she said. "That I haven't killed before."

"Have you?"

"I might have once or twice."

George laughed. "Once or twice? You said it so casually. Do you want to talk about it?"

"Not really, it was in Ron's time, so it's nothing to do with you two."

"It is if it's going to impact us, and if you have a penchant for bumping men off, it *is* impacting us because you're going after Guv. Go on, get it off your chest. You'll feel better afterwards, trust me."

"I've spilled the beans to someone recently and already feel better, so I don't feel the need to go into it all over again."

"What if I want you to? What if you've got no choice?"

He reminded her so much of Ron. "Are you saying I don't?"

George sighed. "Just spit it out, for fuck's sake. It's not like we're going to hold it against you, is it. You're not the type to murder people for no reason."

She studied him to see if he was playing her, but it seemed he was genuinely interested. Maybe Ichabod hadn't said anything after all.

"Well, it isn't very nice, some of the things I did. You're probably going to think I'm a right cow."

"So what if we do? Everyone's done something they're ashamed of and would put them in a bad light, but it's what we do after that, how we behave, that matters. Me and Greg go about doing hideous shit, but we do nice stuff to correct it. You've done nice stuff. You cheer the oldies up at Elm House, not taking any pay. Look how you stood by Amy Osbourne and tried to help her bump Pete off. Most friends would have run a mile if their friend admitted they wanted to kill their old man, but you didn't."

"Because I knew how it felt to be treated like shit, to be beaten up. I knew what it was like to want to stab the shit out of someone."

"Was that how you did it? By stabbing?"

"I used a razor blade. Glued the fucker to a pencil and sliced them up."

George blurted out a short laugh. "A what?"

"A pencil. You can take the piss, but it worked, didn't it?"

"Who did you kill?"

"Two blokes who promised me the world then let me down. Arseholes, the pair of them. Oh, and they were rude to my mum, and that was what set me off."

George smiled. "That's how we get. If anyone bad-mouths our mother, they pay for it. I admire that in you. The devotion you showed when she was ill."

"Yeah, well, I loved her, didn't I." Lil blinked away tears that had sprung up. "I suppose you're going to hold me to ransom and won't help me with Guv until I tell you who I killed?"

"That's about the gist of it. And get a move on. If we're going after him tonight, there's not much left of the day."

Lil took a deep breath. "Get me a triple vodka first, will you?"

"A single. I don't want you off your face on booze at the warehouse, not when brandishing your mighty pencil razor."

"Oh, fuck off." She sighed. "All right, but I'm not saying another word until I've got that drink in my hand."

George stood. "Stubborn old cow."

She glared at him. "Oi, less of the old, you. Now piss off before I change my mind."

Chapter Fifteen

Flint smiled. His current money-making target had skived school this afternoon so she could speak to him without a teacher threatening to confiscate her phone. She called herself Pretty_Hot, and she was, he'd give her that. The photos she'd sent to him so far were disappointing, though. Too much makeup, a trout pout, and her eyebrows brushed upwards and set with gel or whatever so they were spiky. What was that all about? He'd have to push harder in getting her to send a selfie without all that muck on her face. Punters wanted images of girls who looked young.

He chose girls from seeing how they interacted on the main forums. Pretty_Hot liked Xbox-ing the evenings away, so he'd picked the username Gamer_Fiend to lure her in. They'd been talking for a while now, but he needed to move it on. Men messaged him on his secure site on the dark web for new images daily, and while they could download others Flint had already procured, some had already bought them all and wanted 'fresh meat'. He wasn't worried about having the money going into a bank account. He'd set one up used solely for payments, and each transaction was titled something innocent as to which photo they'd bought, like Butterfly on a Leaf or Car by Kerb. The buyers didn't want to get caught any more than Flint did.

So far, it had worked.

GAMER_FIEND: SEND PIC WITH NO MAKEUP.

PRETTY_HOT: NO WAY! [SHOCKED FACE EMOJI]

GAMER_FIEND: WHY NOT? I PREFER GIRLS WITHOUT IT.

PRETTY_HOT: SO WHY ARE YOU TALKING TO ME THEN IF I'M NOT WHAT YOU PREFER? GOD! YOU KNOW I ALWAYS WEAR IT. DON'T WANT ANYONE SEEING ME LOOKING UGLY.

GAMER_FIEND: I BET YOU'RE NOT. SHOW ME.

Flint needed to see whether she seemed a lot younger without any slap on. If she didn't, the image wouldn't sell many copies. He couldn't be doing with wasting any more time on this girl if she wasn't going to be lucrative.

PRETTY_HOT: PROMISE YOU WON'T DITCH ME AFTER?

GAMER_FIEND: I PROMISE.

*IMG_0009_548

She appeared about ten years old. Perfect. She'd said she was out and about until it was time to leave school, otherwise her mum would want to know why she'd come home early. So was this picture from ages ago, before she'd discovered the wonders of foundation and fake eyelashes?

PRETTY_HOT: OH GOD, I KNEW I SHOULDN'T HAVE SENT IT TO YOU. ARE YOU STILL THERE?

GAMER_FIEND: YEP, JUST ADMIRING HOW LOVELY YOU ARE. HONESTLY, DITCH THE MAKEUP. YOU'RE

MUCH HOTTER LIKE THIS. WHEN YOU GO HOME, SCRUB THAT SHIT OFF AND TAKE ANOTHER PIC. SEND IT TO ME.

PRETTY_HOT: ARE YOU SERIOUS?

GAMER_FIEND: YEP. SHOW ME MORE OF YOU, TOO.

PRETTY_HOT: LIKE WHAT?

GAMER_FIEND: TITS? NO BRA. I DARE YOU.

PRETTY_HOT: NO, THEY'RE NOT VERY BIG.

GAMER_FIEND: MY DAD SAID ANY MORE THAN A HANDFUL IS A WASTE.

PRETTY_HOT: YOU WON'T SHOW ANYONE, WILL YOU?

GAMER_FIEND: NO.

Only thousands of men.

Flint opened another can of beer and saved her picture into her file. He had one for each girl he'd spoken to. Screenshots of messages, images, all in case London Teens got shut down for whatever reason. Losing all those pictures would dry his revenue stream right up, plus he liked rereading the conversations.

PRETTY_HOT: OKAY, I TRUST YOU.

GAMER_FIEND: GOOD, I TRUST YOU, TOO. I DON'T TELL EVERYONE ALL THAT SHIT ABOUT MY LIFE.

YOU'RE THE ONLY ONE. THAT MEANS YOU'RE SPECIAL.

PRETTY_HOT: AWW. WHEN CAN WE MEET?

GAMER_FIEND: WHEN I'M NOT GROUNDED. I GOT SUSPENDED FROM SCHOOL, REMEMBER. I'VE GOT TO GO. MUM'S HOME. I'M MEANT TO BE STUDYING.

PRETTY_HOT: OKAY, BYE! WILL SEND PIC LATER. [LOVE HEART EMOJI]

GAMER_FIEND: [THUMBS-UP EMOJI]

He closed the private message thread and clicked out of his username. Browsed his saved chats with a previous girl, Mermaid, then logged in as another user. He spent the next two hours joining in on the forums as Leonardo_Lives, searching for another target in case Pretty_Hot's next image wasn't going to cut the mustard.

Always best to be prepared with a backup plan.

Chapter Sixteen

Guv had scored a job at the factory. It was menial, boring work, but he was used to that from Manchester. It would bring in the readies until either the twins took him on or he found something else. Tonight, he was off to upset Avery again. As she'd have twigged someone had walked straight in last night, he'd bought a tool similar to a lock pick at the little hardware store in town. He'd picked locks numerous times in his life so wasn't fazed, creeping into homes and businesses in the dead of night for Ron, plus the women's places.

After a wander round for a few hours, visiting his old haunts, he returned to his flat and made dinner—well, he microwaved a ready meal and buttered a couple of slices of bread, sorted a cuppa. He sat at the small table in front of the big bay window that looked out onto the street. The flat came sparsely furnished with thick voiles over the panes, and with the light off, he could nose without being seen.

A woman in the ground-floor flat over the road hadn't shut her curtains, and her light was on. She sat on the sofa, the telly flickering opposite, a plate on her lap. In between bites, she used her phone, smiling or laughing. If she wasn't ugly she'd be his side project, something to fill the time after work until he could go into Avery's each night, but her nose was too big, her lips too thin. Still, it was interesting to watch her.

A man walked in, and even if she'd been to Guv's taste, that put paid to him using her as a stopgap. The bloke sat beside her with his dinner, and she put her phone under a nearby pillow in a way where she might not have wanted him to see her doing it. Either her fella didn't like her using it at dinner time, or she'd been messaging someone she shouldn't. Guv liked working out who people were, how they ticked, seeing their lives unfold in front of him, and going by the man sitting so stiffly, these two were going through a rough patch.

That became evident when their mouths moved, then he elbowed her in the cheek. It flung her sideways, her plate falling from her lap onto the sofa, food sliding to the cushion beneath her. He flung his plate across the room, pushing himself up to tower above her. She cowered, hands over her head—so she was used to protecting herself? A punch to the gut sent her mouth wide—a scream coming out?—and he stepped back as though to survey what he'd done. He said something, pointing at her, his finger wagging. She sat up, a hand on her stomach, nodding. The bastard felt beneath the pillow for her phone and prodded the screen. Stared at it. Glanced up at her and dropped it on the floor.

The roundhouse kick to her temple propelled Guv to his feet. He grabbed his keys, shoving them in his pocket, and left his flat, storming across the road, anger burning through him. He jabbed his finger on the bell push for flat one, clenching his fists, ready to fight. A light came on, and a shadow matching the fella's shape walked towards the door.

It opened, and the man glared at him. "Who are you? The bloke she's seeing?"

Guv's adrenaline flared, and his days of working for Ron came to the fore. He thumped the wanker in the face. The arsehole staggered backwards, and Guv entered the communal hallway, laying into him, punching, kicking, until the tosser dropped to the floor in the same pose as the woman on the sofa, hands over his head. A vicious kick to the stomach saw Guv's anger abating, and he stared down at him, breathing heavily.

The woman poked her head out of her flat. "Oh God… Oh shit…" She flicked her attention from her fella to Guv. "What…?"

Guv shrugged. "I saw what he did to you. I live opposite."

She flushed. "Christ…"

"Does he do that often?"

She nodded.

"Do you want it to stop?"

She nodded again.

"Do you want me to make sure it does?"

A third nod.

"Go inside." Guv waited until she'd gone back in then he shut the main door.

He sat on the stairs that led to the upper flat and kept an eye on the prick who writhed in pain. His face, covered in blood, resembled something out of the old days, where Guv had duffed people up without mercy. It pulled out a slew of emotions and memories from when he'd been someone important, feared, and it brought home how much he'd missed being a part of Ron's core team. Too many years of aimlessly going to work in that shitty Manchester factory, the life sucked out of him. How stupid he'd been to follow his need to stalk when his life could have been so brilliant here with Lil.

I never should have left her.

Another groan, this time deep and long. So much for George saying Guv had gone to seed. He still had it in him to give someone a proper good pasting. Maybe that's what the twins needed to see, that he *was* worth taking on, being one of their bullies. He should get them round here so they could assess the damage he'd done.

"Cocks like you don't deserve to live," he said.

"F…fuck you." A spray of blood followed those words.

"Wow, you don't know when you're beaten, do you. But that's all right. I know someone who'll make sure you can't speak properly for weeks." Guv messaged the twins the address, adding:

GUV: IT'S GUV. GOT A WIFE BEATER HERE. I'VE JUST DONE HIM OVER, BUT I THINK HE NEEDS A CHESHIRE. CAN YOU COME AND SEE IF YOU AGREE?

GG: ON OUR WAY.

The man tried to get up, but the kicking had rendered him too weak.

"I wouldn't bother, mate. I'll only knock you back down again."

A glare of hatred answered him. Guv ignored it and sat there for fifteen minutes listening to moans and expletives. The sound of an engine brought him to his feet, and he opened the front door, standing side-on in case the prick had mustered enough energy to get to his feet after his rest.

George and Greg approached in forensic suits—what was that all about?— George coming in first. He stared down at the pathetic waster on the floor and bent to haul him upright. Greg shut the door and stood in front of it, and Guv moved to get the perfect view of the nutter in action.

George shoved the fella onto the stairs and straddled him, knees on each hand pressed to a step. He took a flick-knife from inside his suit and released the long blade, positioning it between the lips and teeth.

"This takes me back to the times when this was all I did along with kneecapping and scaring the shit out of people. It was my job to teach dicks like you a lesson. Ron sent me out to do it—do you know who Ron was? A hard bastard. But not as hard as me, because he preferred guns, the easy way. I like the more painful route. What's your name?"

"E-Eddie." The word sounded odd seeping around the blade: eh-ee.

"Eddie what?"

"Davidson."

"Well, Eddie Davidson, that little bird over there informed me you're a wife beater. Now, in case you want to split hairs, she might not be your wife, she could be your girlfriend or a sister, a cousin, a friend, but I don't much give a fuck, because you laid your hands on her, and that means I need to stop you from doing it again. You know who I am, don't you?"

"Y-yes."

"And you must have been aware that if I found out what you got up to, you'd have to pay the price."

"Yes."

"Yet you did it anyway. Do you know what that tells me? That you're an arrogant cunt who thinks he's above the law—our law. But you're not, and I expect you realise that now."

George pressed the blade. It sliced cleanly through the skin, the cheeks, coming to rest at the back of the gums. Eddie screamed, and it brought someone to the top of the stairs. A blonde woman in her twenties, face a picture of fear.

"Fuck off, there's a good girl," George said, looking up at her. "This is Cardigan business."

She disappeared, and a door slammed, but another opened. Eddie's missus stood peeping through the small gap to the drama playing out behind the banister rails. She appeared half afraid but half happy that a twin had her bloke pinned down. Then her eyes widened, possibly at the claret, the knife. Guv switched his attention from her to the stairs. Blood, there was a lot of it, streaming from the slices to meander down the neck. George gave the knife an extra push, and Eddie's screech reached ear-splitting levels.

"Shut up!" George shouted. "Shut the fuck up!" He removed the knife, wiped it on his white suit, and pressed a button. The blade retracted, and he slid it away.

Eddie sobbed, tears dripping down to merge with the blood.

"You're going to go to the hospital and say you were attacked on your way home. Some mad bastard nicked your wallet. You'll be sewn up, and coppers will come to speak to you, but you have no idea who did this to you. If you tell them it was me, I'll find out who your family is and fucking kill them, understand? You won't come back here again. You won't bother the lady in that flat. She'll bag your stuff up, and we'll drop it round your mum's house. Do you have a mum?"

Eddie nodded.

"She'll be made to understand why your face has got an extra smile. She'll be paid for her silence. Hopefully, she'll be so disgusted by you that she won't let you kip in her spare room. I'm imagining you being homeless, wandering around. But because of the state of your face, everyone will know it was me, and everyone will know you must have done something bad to deserve it. People will turn a blind eye and won't put money in your begging pot. So you're better off making yourself scarce, leaving London, because no leader will want you on their manor. I'll put the word out. So be a sensible lad and fuck off out of here. You're not welcome anymore."

George grabbed him by the T-shirt and dragged him off the stairs. Marched him to the door. Greg opened it, and George threw Eddie outside. It had been a masterpiece of menace, and Guv now understood why he'd been warned that the twins were worse than Ron. Or George was. There was something eerie about the big man and his actions, it hadn't just been a slice to the face but an orchestrated ritual, and it downright gave Guv the creeps. As did Greg just standing there, observing.

Fuck me sideways…

George came back in and shut the door. He looked over at the woman. "You all right, love?"

"Yes," she whispered.

"Get his stuff packed up. Someone will come and collect it. He shouldn't be bothering you again. But if he does, ring us." He drew down his suit zip and brought out a business card and an envelope. Blood from his gloves smeared them. "You'll need to burn these once you've taken down our number and removed the cash. I got them a bit dirty." Going over to her, he put them in her hand. "Buy yourself something nice to take the taste of that tosser away. You saw nothing, understand? A couple of people will be by in half an hour or so to wash the blood off the stairs, so make sure his gear's ready by then so they can get rid of it. Have a nice evening." He stalked outside, stepping over Eddie on the path. "Are you still here, my old son? Can't you get up? Let me help you into our van. I've changed my mind about you. You're not going to the hospital."

Guv glanced at Greg. "Jesus."

Greg smiled. "He teaches a hard lesson, eh?"

"Too right. Well, I'd best get back to my dinner." Guv went outside to the sound of Eddie mumbling something and George telling him to shut his bastard face.

Greg followed, closing the door. "What were you doing here, Guv? Passing by?"

"Nah, I live opposite. Saw her being beaten up through the window."

"Right, well, see you around."

Guv nodded and crossed the street. In his flat, he sat at the table and watched the van drive away, then swerved his attention to the flat over the road. The woman was on her phone again, perhaps messaging whoever had made her smile and laugh before. Her bit on the side? Then she got on with cleaning the mess, the broken plate, the food. She wiped her eyes with the back of her hand at one point, standing there with her shoulders shaking.

It seemed this was the end of a long road for her.

Guv nodded. He'd done the right thing for once.

His phone bleeped, and he checked the message.

LIL: EIGHT O'CLOCK AT THE RED LION?

Guv thought about that for a few seconds. While he needed Lil as his cover, the person who'd give him an air of respectability and innocence, it could wait. He wanted to see Avery more.

GUV: TOMORROW NIGHT INSTEAD? JUST BEEN WITH THE TWINS WHILE GEORGE DEALT OUT A CHESHIRE. ADRENALINE RUSH, SO I'M KNACKERED. SORRY.

LIL: BLIMEY. OKAY, TOMORROW IT IS THEN. LET ME KNOW WHAT TIME.

GUV: WILL DO.

He switched his phone to silent and finished his cold food. The woman collected bits and bobs from around the living room and put them in a carrier bag. Eddie's things.

Clearing the table and taking his plate and untouched tea to the kitchen, he washed up, thinking of Avery and that cup and glass. The creepy music.

Would she have phoned the police?

Time would tell.

At eleven o'clock, Guv stood in the shield of the same two trees he'd hidden between last night. Avery sat at her table again, the laptop open in front of her. She'd been on it for an hour, getting up twice to smoke a cigarette at the open kitchen window. She kept glancing outside, probably to check if anyone was there. If she'd realised those French doors had been unlocked last night, she'd know whoever had entered her house had done so through those. She was being sensible, not coming outside to smoke, but why the hell, if he'd scared her as much as he'd hoped, did she have the curtains and blind open? Was she into torturing herself by having that feeling of eyes on her?

She rose, going over to a coffee machine and putting her cup beneath the spout. She added a pod then went back to the table to pick up her cigarettes. Stood in front of the sink unit to blow the smoke outside. She bit her bottom lip, alternating between staring out and looking at the floor, pensive, pondering. What was she thinking? Had he unnerved her with what he'd done? Did she wish she didn't live alone?

Her phone rang, and she rushed to collect it from the table, walking back over to the window to answer it, her head down.

Guv crept out of the trees and whipped across the garden to stand between the window and doors.

"Yes, I'm fine. Too wired to sleep, though, so I'm doing a bit of work. The Brothers came earlier."

What the fuck?

What had they done that for? Yes, a fire had broken out on their patch, but there wasn't any need for them to get involved. Unless they ran things completely different to Ron, wanting to get to the bottom of everything. Did they actually *care* about what happened to their residents? And how had they even found out who Avery was?

"Yeah, they wanted to check whether I'd killed Pax, and if it was justified, they'd help me get away with it... I know people say they're monsters, but honestly, I saw a different side to them today. They know it wasn't me, yes... Hmm, they knew the police were coming round as well. They must have a copper who tells them stuff. Makes sense, because they get away with a lot of shit. Anyway, a woman called Odelle came...no, Odette, that's it, and she wanted to know how my last date with Pax had gone and when I'd last seen him." A pause. "Of *course* I told her. I've got no reason to lie." Another pause where she listened. "Apparently, the fire started from a cigarette, and the police thought it had been an accident, but the post-mortem showed he had broken legs, so they're now treating it as murder."

Fucking hell… I made a mistake there.

"I know. Who the hell would have done that? Yeah, I told them you'd come round just after Pax left and you stayed the night. I told the copper that, too, and she wanted your name and address, so maybe she wants to speak to you, confirm my alibi or whatever. I also said about the washing up and Alexa. The Brothers said I ought to get CCTV, so I nipped to town and got one of those cheap little cameras."

Guv's guts rolled. He closed his eyes, cursing himself for being so blasé about tonight. Okay, he'd put on a beanie, pulling a face mask up as soon as he'd entered the garden, but… He thought back to when he'd cut across the garden to the trees upon his arrival. He'd purposely skirted around the splashes of square light on the grass, keeping to the shadowed areas. Maybe he'd be safe from detection on the camera at that point, but he'd fucked up just now, not giving thought to anything except listening to her talking. If The Brothers saw any footage, they'd know it was him, surely.

"I've put it on the sideboard behind my dining room table, pointing towards the doors. No, it doesn't chime or anything if it picks someone up, the bloke in the shop said it isn't that sophisticated, but I've been there all night and haven't seen anyone outside… Well, yes, I have been to the loo, but there's no one out there, I swear. No, don't come over, I'll be okay. I'm going to bed after a coffee anyway, not that I'll be able to sleep."

Smoke wafted out of the window. Guv fished for his vape in a pocket and chugged on it, blowing the vapour downwards into the dark. The act of smoking calmed him a little but not enough to eradicate all of his nerves. He ought to abandon Avery and find someone else. But what he *ought* to do and what his stupid mind told him to do were two different matters.

"No, I've taken the rest of the week off work. This has all been a bit much. What? No, Odette doesn't think I did it, thank God. She knew all about Just Dates so is looking into the other women. Two of them had reported him for stalking, can you believe that? No, nothing was done, which doesn't surprise me, sadly. Anyway, I'd better let you go. I'll message you in the morning so you know I'm still alive." She laughed but sounded worried.

The window slammed shut.

Guv didn't bother going back to the trees. He ducked beneath the window and crouch-walked to the edge of the house. Used stealth when going down the side. He checked the street. Giving himself the all-clear, he dipped his head and sloped away, pissed off he couldn't go in the house soon and fuck with Avery's mind.

Unless he returned in an hour or two…

Chapter Seventeen

Mum was ill. She'd been suffering for a couple of years, eventually going to the doctors three days ago, convinced the menopause was being particularly brutal to her. The ME diagnosis explained why she winced when moving because of the painful joints, why she was so tired, and why she had difficulty drawing on memories or concentrating. Some of the neighbours had called it Yuppie Flu, and Lil had taken them down a peg or two, explaining it wasn't the fucking flu but an actual illness, you nasty bunch of tarts. She'd insisted Mum gave up work. The laundrette brought in more than enough, and Lil had bagged herself some regular sets in pubs on another Estate, actually getting paid for it each Saturday night.

In the kitchen, she closed the door, Mum now settled in her favourite chair, so Lil didn't mind leaving her alone. Not now she'd accepted her diagnosis, seeming brighter. Lil didn't think she'd *be bright if someone told her she was ill and it could get worse, but Mum had said it was because what was wrong with her now had a name, she wasn't imagining all those symptoms, and she'd gone on HRT patches while she was at it. She wasn't happy about leaving the workload to Lil, the responsibility to feed them and pay the bills, but she'd just have to get used to it. Mum had looked after Lil all her life, and Lil would return the favour for the rest of Mum's.*

Guv appeared at the back door, and she jumped. She'd finally given in, taking him at his word, and he'd proved he wasn't some dodgy tosser only doing Ron's bidding. In fact, she'd brought out her rose-coloured glasses again, only one lens tinted pink, though, the other clear as a bell to remind her that he could change in a flash. But three years was a long time to keep up appearances, and he hadn't once slipped up.

Mind you, that was a lie. Some nights, after he'd been out and about for Ron, Guv came back jumpy, ratty, but he always warned her he wasn't in the best of moods so she could retreat. He didn't want to bite her head off. She'd got it into her head he was having an affair, doing each job then nipping to see some woman afterwards. Granted, he must think it was weird, having sex with Lil when Mum was in the same house, and Lil hadn't gone to his flat all that often when he'd had it. She certainly hadn't taken him to the cottage or even let him know it existed, but…

Was she being silly?

No, before she got any deeper with him, she had to be certain their relationship was solid. Ron had ensured she trusted no man, and if there were niggles, then it meant her gut was warning her something was off. If she didn't listen, then on her own head be it.

She unlocked the door and let Guv in. "What did you come round the back for?"

"I saw your mum through the front window. She had her eyes shut, so…"

"Thanks for being thoughtful. She's so tired all the time."

She couldn't fault him on that, being kind. He was great with her mother, respectful, and he asked her to join them on dates every now and then. On any Saturday nights he didn't have a job for Ron, he sat with Mum in pubs while Lil sang. Those times were the best, Mum so bloody proud, telling everyone around her that her daughter was the singer, and wasn't she amazing?

"How has she been today?" he asked. "You know, after the bombshell."

"Perkier. It's because she now knows what to do to alleviate her symptoms, and when she has a crash, as the doctor called it, she has to rest instead of pushing through it like she did before. I've got some leaflets and a book to read because I want to know all about it so I can help her."

"I'll read them, too." Guv sat at the table, elbows propped on top, his forehead in his hands.

"Sleepy?" she asked.

"Hmm."

"Maybe all those late nights are catching up with you. Sometimes you don't get in until gone four o'clock."

He raised his head. "Keeping tabs on me?" His grin took away any rancour.

"I think you clattering about and waking me up might have been a clue that you got in late."

"Sorry. Maybe I should have kept my place on. I could have kipped there and not disturbed you."

That tied in with her suspicious thoughts, and she stiffened. What if he'd said that so if he got a new flat, she wouldn't think it was anything iffy?

"Maybe." She glanced at the digital display on the microwave. Four p.m. She had almost two hours to spare. "Anyway, I'd best get the dinner on, I've got to be at the laundrette for six."

Since Guv mainly worked at night and had his days free, Lil had altered her schedule to fit. Plus, now Mum didn't have to work, Lil could care for her in the daytime and rest easy on the weekday evenings at the laundrette. Her staff did the weekends.

Lil wasn't coming home after work tonight. She had a plan in mind, and it involved getting Guv to nip to the laundrette and her following him after he'd left. She'd have to time it just right, get him to come to the back entrance, but if she put this suspicion to bed, they'd be golden.

That time last month prodded at her again. He'd come back one night covered in blood, which wasn't that surprising, given that he worked for Ron. They'd whispered in the dark after his shower, him stiff as a board beside her in bed. He'd said he had to kill someone called Reginald who was a drug dealer giving Ron all kinds of gyp. Except Guv felt bad about it, said the fella had three kids and he reckoned Ron had got his wires crossed—that Reginald was the wrong target.

Lil had texted Ron the next morning, asking him about the job.

RON: WHO THE FUCK IS REGINALD NOAKES?

LIL: WHO INDEED.

RON: IF HE'S OFFING PEOPLE WITHOUT MY SAY-SO, I'LL FUCKING HAVE HIM.

LIL: LEAVE IT WITH ME. I'LL KEEP TABS AND LET YOU KNOW WHETHER I FIND ANYTHING ELSE OUT.

RON: IF HE TURNS OUT LIKE JAKE AND BOD…

LIL: AT LEAST THIS TIME I CAN'T BLAME YOU FOR PICKING HIM FOR ME. UNLESS YOU DID?

RON: THAT WAS SOD ALL TO DO WITH ME. I WAS SURPRISED ABOUT IT TO BE FAIR.

LIL: RIGHT. I'LL GET HOLD OF YOU IF ANYTHING CROPS UP.

RON: IF YOU NEED THE STEEL ROOM, YOU MEAN. I NOTICED YOU HAVEN'T BEEN TO THE COTTAGE.

LIL: I TOLD YOU I WOULDN'T GO THERE.

RON: I MISS YOU.

LIL: FUCK OFF, RON.

Lil locked the laundrette's front door and switched the lights off. In the staffroom, she popped on her coat, hung her bag strap on her shoulder. The notes the customers exchanged for coins so they could use the machines were scattered on the floor, along with a few fifty-pence pieces, the odd ten p, and the till tray. Everything was set up, so she texted Guv.

LIL: SOMEONE'S JUST TRIED TO ROB THE LAUNDRETTE.

GUV: WHAT? CHRIST, I'M FIVE MINUTES AWAY. RING THE POLICE.

LIL: NO! I DON'T WANT THIS GETTING OUT ELSE ALL THE SCROTES WILL COME AND HAVE A POP AS WELL. HURRY UP. COME ROUND THE BACK.

She waited, sitting at the little table, glancing around to make sure the stage she'd set appeared genuine. She got lost inside her head, going through the next stage. A hard tap at the back door brought on a smile—he'd made it here in three minutes, so he must have run if his job didn't require a car, or he'd floored it in one of the stolen vehicles Ron regularly acquired.

She got up and unlocked the door—the type that didn't need locking from outside when she left. "Thank fuck you're here. This has shit me right up."

Guv came in and stared at the money. "Why wasn't that till tray in the safe?"

"I popped it on the table so I could have a quick wee…"

"Have you checked everywhere? No one's about?"

"Yes, and no. I caught him just as he was picking the tray up. He panicked, dropped it, and legged it."

Guv stooped to pick everything up. "Did you get a look at his face?"

"No, he had something over the bottom half. A bandana, I think, but it was a kid, I'm sure of it."

Guv handed her the tray. "Get that put away. I may as well go for a slash while I'm here." He went into the little toilet and shut the door.

Lil had been making mental notes during their interaction.

He'd blamed her immediately by asking why the money hadn't been put away, implying her incompetence had led to the robbery—someone could have looked through the window beside the door, seen the cash, and chanced their arm.

He'd taken her word no one was here instead of double-checking himself—her safety wasn't uppermost in his mind.

He'd gone to the loo instead of asking the first question that should have come out of his mouth: Are you all right?

Okay, all that could be put down to him being analytical, assessing the scene first, and emotions might come into it once he'd had a wee, but it would come too late for her. The three red flags waved in the breeze her gut instinct created, but she filed it for now.

She put the tray away, saddened she wasn't top of his list.

Guv emerged, going straight to the back door. "I've got to go. Ron's going to go mental if he finds out I left the job."

"What were you doing?"

"Scoping a man's place out. Drugs again."

He disappeared, and she switched off the light and quickly followed, leaning on the door as it closed behind her so she could control any noise. His shape in the darkness of the alley guided her, and he walked out into the light of a streetlamp. He turned right, and Lil went after him, staying back enough that if he saw her, he'd think she was walking home, but he'd wonder why when she'd come here in the Mini.

Another red flag: He hadn't suggested driving her home in her car parked out the front. Instead, he'd left her to any dangers, the robber lurking in the darkness waiting to grab her. His mind was clearly on Ron's job and she didn't factor.

He went through town, then on a few streets, and she frowned when he stopped outside a house in Princeton Avenue. Noelle's house. No, she couldn't allow him to do anything to that woman, and there was Hailey, who'd be about three now. The gossip-vine hadn't hummed with news of Noelle having a new fella, and she wasn't the sort to be in any trouble, so why would Guv have to target her house?

He moved along, dipped down the alley between two homes, vanishing in the darkness. Lil tailed him, relieved to see the top of his silhouette, the dark-grey sky of night the backdrop. He took a left—thank God, it meant Noelle wasn't involved—and she tiptoed along the alley. Out at the other end, she stared ahead. Where had he gone?

Lil crept past the high wooden fences at the bottom of the gardens and stopped to peer through knotholes. She found him three houses along. Finding a gap where the gate slats didn't meet, she strained to see through. He stood to the right on the grass, staring inside at a woman who sat at her kitchen table. He'd said he was scoping a man's house out—God, she hoped he didn't have to hurt the bloke's missus, or was that a daughter?

She didn't want to watch any violence but remain rooted. The woman got up and switched the light off. Guv stayed in place. Time seemed to slow, and Lil was getting cold, but she wanted to know what was going on. What Guv would do.

He made his move, going to the back door and crouching. He appeared to be doing something to the lock, and when the door opened, she guessed he'd used a pick. Inside now, he closed the door. A light came on—he had a torch, a small one, going by the width of the beam which flashed around. Another light, showcasing the inside of a fridge. He reached inside, moving things around, and an awful, terrible feeling swamped Lil's belly.

The East End Stalker did that. He moved things in fridges.

Then Guv put his torch down, the shaft of light from it pointing towards a cooker, and took something out of the fridge, his back keeping the door open. He peeled a wrapper off the top of something, a plastic tub, then popped whatever was inside in his mouth. A strawberry?

Lil relaxed a bit. He wasn't the Stalker after all, just moving things so he could find something to eat. But that was weird in itself, breaking into a target's home and scoffing their food. In her head, she removed the rose-coloured lens and replaced it with a clear one to match the other so her vision, and her emotions, were free of the encumbrance loving someone brought—and she did love him. He was good to her and Mum, but…

The fridge door closed, and he must have picked up the torch because the light flickered around again. Then it wasn't there, so he'd gone deeper into the house. Should she go after him? If this really was just a job for Ron, she'd be in a lot of shit for meddling, but if it wasn't…

She turned tail and ran, away from something that could be so bad she'd never get over it, and she kept going until she got home. She checked on Mum, getting into bed afterwards, trying to control the shakes. She should ring Ron, tell him her suspicions, but they could just be her stupid mind adding things up, the total the completely wrong number.

She reached out for her phone on the nightstand and, lying on her side, prodded at the keys.

LIL: WHO IS GUV GOING AFTER TONIGHT?

The reply didn't come for a while.

RON: HE HASN'T GOT A JOB TONIGHT. WHY?

LIL: DOESN'T MATTER.

But it did, it mattered a lot.

Guv had lied to her.

Chapter Eighteen

Avery woke at eleven a.m. after a fitful night where she hadn't gone into a proper sleep until five. She'd read her Kindle, although at times it had hit her in the face when she'd dropped off. A check of the clock always showed she'd barely shut her eyes for seconds.

She crawled out of bed, bashing her toe on the corner of a chest of drawers. Rubbing her watering eyes and cursing the pain—why did a stubbed toe always feel worse than anything else?—she wandered onto the landing and checked the spare bedroom. Was this her life now, making sure no one had got inside? Would this be her ritual every bloody morning?

Nothing appeared out of place in there, so she had a shower. While drying herself, she frowned at the sink. She always put her electric toothbrush beside the cold tap and the paste beside the hot. They were the wrong way round. It wouldn't usually have bothered her, she'd have thought she'd been preoccupied with her thoughts last night when she'd brushed her teeth, but she distinctly remembered putting the paste on the correct side because she'd spotted one of her hairs and had swilled it with water to send it down the plughole.

Chilled with shivers of dread, she quickly brushed her teeth and put things the right way round. She hung the towel up and dressed in her room, looking about to see if anything was off in there. All seemed okay, so she picked up her phone and went downstairs, bracing herself for what she might find.

One of her high-heeled shoes next to the front door lay on its side, but that could have fallen over by itself. Still, it bothered her, and she checked the living room, her heartbeat going a bit too fast. A photo on the windowsill had fallen onto its front, the image hidden—Avery and her parents on holiday last year. She'd shut the curtains last night, yet they were open. Her remote controls were on the sofa, but she always put them away in the little cubby holder she'd bought from Amazon.

She shivered again and left the room, dreading going into the kitchen. Phone clutched tight, she was about to ring The Brothers, but she spotted three coins on the floor in the hallway. A pound, a fifty pence, and a penny. They butted against each other, forming a sort of triangle. If they'd come out of her purse, they'd have been more scattered, and she'd have known they'd fallen out because she'd have heard them hitting the floor. But she hadn't even *touched* her purse yesterday. Had the twins or Odette dropped them?

That didn't explain their placement, though.

Freaked out, Avery skirted past and checked the kitchen. Nothing was out of place there, and she calmed herself down. All the misplaced things could have happened naturally, couldn't they? Be put down to her tiredness, her not thinking straight, and although she was creeped out, she'd have a cigarette and a coffee, then get hold of the twins, let them decide whether this shit was weird or not.

But it *was* weird, she couldn't deny it.

She stuck a pod in the machine and added milk and sweetener to a cup. Window open, she lit a cigarette and stared into the garden. All was okay out there, too, but she'd consider having a new gate put in down the side, one of those tall ones she could lock. Someone could climb over it, but at least she might hear them doing that and could call for help before they got into her house.

Fag finished, she opened the fridge to put the milk away and blinked at the middle shelf. Why hadn't she seen that when she'd taken the milk out? A casserole dish with a glass lid, one she'd put there after making a stew and letting it cool yesterday, wasn't in the same place. The lid was partially off, the edge propped on a tub of margarine that was usually on the shelf above. A tin of beans—she never put open tins in there, Mum said it could make you poorly—sat beside the dish, a teaspoon sticking out of it.

If terror was a colour, it would be white. It streaked through her, so cold, and she fumbled putting the milk in the bottle section of the door.

She slammed the fridge and backed away, tears burning. Phone snatched up, she pressed GG in her message app and managed to poke in a text, her hand shaking.

AVERY: SOMEONE'S BEEN IN MY HOUSE! THINGS HAVE BEEN MOVED.

She swiped to her home page and accessed the camera app. Several recordings had saved, which meant it had detected movement. That could be her getting up and walking past it, and many stills were of the lit dining area. But two were not. One was of the French doors, blackness beyond, squares of light on the grass, a dark trainer and the bottom of a leg at the edge of one top square. The other was of a person, in a pose as if he was running, right in the middle of the squares. She sucked in a sharp breath, her head going fuzzy, and she had to lean against the cooker, her legs weakening. Nauseated, she pressed PLAY on that one. A man in a mask shot out of the trees across the garden. She watched the other video, which only showed the foot appearing and a dark mass in the night, possibly the shape of him, then the shadows of the trees shimmering in the squares of light on the right-hand side.

"Fuck. *Fuck*! Oh God. Oh fucking hell…"

She messaged again.

AVERY: THE CAMERA CAUGHT A MAN IN MY GARDEN!

GG: HOLD TIGHT. ALREADY EN ROUTE. FIVE MINUTES AWAY.

Avery lit a cigarette and opened the window. She reached across for her coffee, calmer now the twins were coming but still shitting herself. Who was the man? Was this a case of mistaken identity and he thought she was someone else? She'd only lived here for three months. Was he connected to the woman who'd sold it to her?

She put her coffee down and looked at the times on the footage. For the one with just the trainer, she'd been sitting at the table, but going by a cross-reference with the second video and the time Louise had phoned, Avery had been here, at the kitchen window. Where had he gone after he'd run across the garden? Had he ducked under the window? The thought of him doing that when she'd had no idea set her off crying.

Maybe she should go and stay with her mum and dad in Ealing for a while. Take next week off work so the twins could do whatever it was they did in these situations. Her boss had already given her the rest of this week off, understanding why Avery was so upset and couldn't concentrate.

She stubbed her fag out and lit another. Drank her coffee. Made another.

The doorbell chimed, and she jumped, letting out a stupid, pathetic screech. She dodged past the coins on the floor and checked through the peephole. The twins. More tears erupted, and she drew the chain and bolts across, flinging the door open, never so glad to see anyone in her life.

"Christ, love, you look like a bag of hammers. Out of the way so we can come in." George brushed past her and ran upstairs.

Greg entered and went into the living room. Avery poked her head out into the street and glanced left and right. No one sat in cars or watched her from windows. She shut the door and found Greg in the kitchen. It sounded as though George was even going up in the loft, the screech of the ladder loud.

"Did you see the money?" She hugged herself and nodded at the hallway floor.

Greg stared over at it. "Why the fuck would someone put that there?" He nosed through the French doors. "Don't tell me anything until George comes back down. Saves you repeating yourself."

Despite feeling sick, Avery lit another cigarette. "This is doing my nut in."

The clonk of footsteps stopped her from saying anything further. George walked along the hallway, stopped, and gazed down at the coins.

"Err, what? That's a bit random." He came over and held his arms out. "You look like you need one, but if you're not a hugger, tell me to fuck off."

She let him cuddle her, closing her eyes, wishing this shit wasn't happening.

"Tell us all about it. Greg can make us drinks."

Avery didn't usually smoke away from the window or doors, but fuck it, she found an old chipped cup to use as an ashtray, filled the bottom with water, and sat at the table. She started from the beginning, the toothbrush and paste, and recalled her walk through the house. "It shits me up that I didn't hear him coming upstairs. I was awake until five, but he was here long before then because of the time stamp on the videos."

"Did you have the telly on or anything?"

"No, I was reading my Kindle. I didn't hear a bloody thing. I did drop off a couple of times, but only for seconds. I had my bedroom door shut, so maybe that was why I didn't pick up on anything."

"Have you checked the back doors yet?"

"No. I didn't think to. I was too upset about all the other stuff going on."

George got up and turned the handles. "Locked. So he must have used a pick and secured it after he left. Show me the footage."

Avery got it up on her phone and passed it to him, thanking Greg for the coffee he brought over. He collected the other two cups then sat, staring outside.

"Fucking cunt," George muttered. "But he made the mistake of running across the garden." He handed Greg the phone. "Makes me wonder whether he got spooked, or maybe he was too intent on getting past these doors to listen to your phone call, and being careful went out of the window. Greg, who does that remind you of? Look at the eyes."

Greg's face muscles tightened. "Shit. So he might well have had something to do with Pax."

Avery's heart thudded. "What? Who?"

George picked his cup up. "Do you know anyone called The Guv'nor?"

"No… What's he got to do with Pax?"

George explained who The Guv'nor was and that he'd been discussing the fire with the landlord of a pub. It didn't make sense. If he'd killed Pax, why was he bothering *her*? Had he followed their taxi after dates? What for?

She shook her head. "I don't get this at all."

"Neither do I," George said, "but I'm almost sure this is Guv, and we know where he lives, so we'll pick him up shortly. We'll let you know when he's been taken care of. In the meantime, can we drop you off anywhere, at someone's house so you're safe?"

Avery nodded. She decided against bothering her parents. "I'll ring Louise. She's at work, but I have a key to her place. I just need to let her know I'm going there."

George looked at Greg. "I'm going to hurt that bastard so badly."

"You and me both, bruv."

Chapter Nineteen

Frustrated as fuck, George couldn't think of anywhere else Guv might be other than one of the many pubs or the factory. If he'd got a job in the latter, he could have started today, hence why he seemed AWOL. He wasn't at his flat, but while in his street, they nipped over the road to check on the poor cow from last night, plus give her another monetary sweetener.

George pressed the bell push for her flat and glanced at Greg. "If you were her, would you go to work the day after someone had lumped you one?"

"No, not if it fucked with my head, but she might have to keep her mind off seeing that Cheshire and whatnot. Not everyone's like you. They don't get pleasure out of blood and gore."

They'd had her looked into. Freya Michaels, twenty-four. Beauty consultant. Mason had found out something odd regarding Guv, too, letting them know in a phone call after they'd left Avery's. He appeared to have dropped off the face of the earth. His real name, which might be why he'd called himself The Guv'nor, was Benedict Rufus Stallworth (not many of those to the pound), and it hadn't come up in any searches since the day he'd left London.

Something must have happened for Ron to let Guv go incognito, telling people he was dead, and before George killed him, he wanted to know the full truth of it. Other than Lil's stalking and killing suspicion, what else could it be? *Had* Ron known, though? That bastard had claimed to adore his wife yet had Treacles on the side, impregnating some of them. He used and abused, discarding them when another young thing caught his eye, so he wasn't exactly a supporter of women in the right way. If he'd found out Guv was what had been known as the East End Stalker (Mason had dug deep), he might have covered it up. Told Guv to fuck off and never come back.

Mason had found a lot of newspaper articles. The East End Stalker had moved things in women's homes, always leaving three coins of various denominations on the floor. If that wasn't proof enough that Guv was the culprit, along with that footage from Avery's garden and the coins and weird shit going on at hers, George didn't know what was. The same thing had been going on in Manchester, the coins being the main thing that had stood out, his name up there the Coin Creep, bestowed on him by the press. Over thirty single women had reported someone breaking into their homes over the years he'd been there, and unfortunately, five of them had been killed.

Guv had a lot to answer for. Avery was his next target, and George had no plans to let him continue his bad habits.

The door opened, drawing him out of his head. Freya stood there, her eyes going wide upon seeing them.

"Afternoon," George said. A lot of the day had swept by, what with seeing Avery earlier then searching for the elusive Guv. "Just need a quick chat."

She stepped back to allow them in, wandering down the shared foyer to her front door. George went in after her, Greg tailing behind. She waited in a little hallway, two doors on either side. She entered the first room on the left, taking them into a lounge that faced the street.

"Mind if we sit?" George eyed the sofa. A stain, perhaps a watermark on the green fabric, had him rethinking his question. "Is that dry?"

"Should be," she said. "I had to wash it last night because…because I spilled my dinner on it."

"You spilled it, or Eddie did something that made it spill?"

"Eddie…" She lowered onto one end of the sofa. "Is he okay? I mean…"

George frowned. "Are you seriously asking if that cunt's all right after what he did to you?" Was she still in that phase where her abuser had mental control over her, even when he was out of the picture? He had to tread carefully—thoughts of Mum crowded in, how she'd put up with Richard bashing her about because Ron had forced her to suffer. Mum had been made of strong stuff, but Freya might not be.

She fiddled with her fingers. "Sorry, I…"

"Don't say sorry. It's not your job to take the blame because he walloped you."

"It is. I… I've been chatting to someone else behind his back. Eddie had got suspicious. He saw my phone last night and…he was upset."

"Right, but that doesn't justify what he did. You've probably been talking to someone else because the situation with Eddie got so bad—it's not unusual to find solace elsewhere, it's been happening forever. How many other times did he get upset over the small things? How many times did you tell yourself that if you'd just straightened the curtains, if you'd made sure the flat was always tidy, if you'd cooked the dinner better, if you *breathed* right, everything would be okay?"

"He likes things nice."

"I'm sure he did, but you need to understand, *none of this is your fault*. Some men want to control everything. I'm one of them, but I'd never lay a hand on an innocent woman. I've killed guilty ones, I'll admit that, but punching them for the fun of it? Nah." He took a card out of his pocket. "Go and see Vic. He's our therapist; it won't cost you a penny. He'll show you how to get through this and come out the other side. Eddie's dead, just so you know. I sliced him into ribbons last night then chopped him up. His body won't be found. He'll never hurt you again."

Maybe that was a bit much, a bit too soon. Tears sprang up and fell down her cheeks, and her lips wobbled.

"I hoped you'd do that, but I feel so bad about it." She stared at the floor. "I just…the man I've been speaking to, he told me Eddie wasn't normal, the things he did, and I could see that in the end, but it's still a mess up here." She tapped the side of her head. "He fucked me over so much I'm worried I won't *get* to the other side of it."

"You will. Now listen, do you have anything to do with his family?"

"Not really."

"But they know you exist?"

"Yes."

"If they come round asking you where he is, say he walked out, he left you, and you don't know where he's gone. He took all his stuff. If they contact the police and report him missing, you say the same thing to any coppers." He paused. "The woman upstairs. Do you know her?"

"Charlotte? She's at work but popped by this morning to see if I was okay. She won't say anything. She knows what Eddie's like."

That brought Lil and Amy to mind, then Stacey and Hailey, how they'd leaned on each other for support over men who'd been abusive. Women were unique like that, some kind of girl code where they propped the other up in times of distress. Plotted, schemed, tried to make things right, even if it *did* mean committing murder.

George took two envelopes out. "The thicker one's for you. I know I gave you some cash last night, but I was thinking about it, and it wasn't enough, considering what you saw. A bit horrific, I'm sure, although I quite like blood and guts. Anyway, take yourself on a nice holiday or something, get a bit of sun—but not for a while, else it'll look like you're running, hiding. The other one's for Charlotte. Tell her from me that if she opens her gob, we'll be back round. I'm sure she'll catch my drift."

"She will. She recognised you so…yeah."

"Have you seen the bloke who beat Eddie up since last night?"

"He went out early this morning. I was talking to Charlotte at the main front door so I could double-lock it after she left. Eight o'clock, something like that. Her flat's got two floors, so it's just us two who live here. I didn't know Eddie was dead and worried he'd come back. I saw the man late last night, too. He'd come home from somewhere."

From being in Avery's garden, the bastard.

"Thanks for that. Is Eddie's name on the tenancy?"

"No, he didn't live here, just stayed over a few times a week. The cleaning ladies, the ones you sent to wash the stairs, I gave them his bits and pieces, clothes and stuff. But I've been worrying. His phone's going to show he was here."

"It's also going to show that when that phone left with our cleaners, it went to the Thames a few miles away. That's the last place Eddie was, if you know what I mean. Does he have a car we need to get rid of?"

"No, he gets a taxi here."

"Okay, well, as far as you're concerned, you didn't see him get into a cab when he walked out because you were crying at your relationship being over. You loved him and were well upset. Do you understand?"

She sniffed. Nodded. "What if the police don't believe me?"

"*Make* them. Who's the bloke you've been speaking to on the side?"

"A man I work with. Wesley Goode."

"He'd better be fucking good to you an' all else he'll have me to deal with. Tell him you've become mates with us today, proper friendly, just to be on the safe side. Let him know how Eddie fared." He smiled. "We'll be off, then. Give us a bell if things go tits up with the police, if they even come round. We might be able to smooth it out. There's this copper we know…"

She stood. "I get it."

They left, Freya locking the main front door behind them, even though there was no fear of Eddie coming back. It pissed George off that whatever that fucker had done to her, it was still ingrained and would likely take months or years for her to get over it. But there was Mr Goode.

Hopefully he'd turn out to be a nice fella. If he wasn't, he'd end up in the same boat as Eddie.

On the way to the BMW, George sent a message to Mason, asking him to poke into Goode, see if he had any secrets. If he did, there'd be words in his ear to keep away from Freya.

In the car, George buckled up.

Greg got in the driver's seat and stared over at Guv's flat. "The factory?"

"Yeah."

"I was watching his flat while we were with Freya, and he hasn't come back." Greg drove away. "That poor cow reminded me of Mum."

"I know what you mean."

"Some men need stringing up for the way they treat women."

"Yep. Where do you reckon Guv will be if he hasn't started work today?"

"Your guess is as good as mine."

George let his mind drift to what he'd said to Freya about killing women. Had she taken that as him implying he'd kill *her* if she didn't say and do what she'd been told? The last thing he wanted was for her to torment herself with thoughts of being offed. He really didn't engage his brain sometimes before he said stuff.

Do better. Think before putting your foot in it.

Greg pulled in around the back of the factory, the car park full of employee vehicles. They got out and entered via the staff door. It led to a small room, a woman sitting at the back, the whole section cordoned off by a counter and a glass partition on top that had a sliding piece in the middle. It looked new and puzzled George. Did the staff get bolshy so she had to keep herself safe? The factory owner paid protection money, and if lairy shit was going on, George needed to know about it.

"Why are you in there?" he asked.

She widened her eyes in recognition, then seemed confused, as if wondering whether they were here to collect this week's payment when Martin usually did it. "Oh, we had someone come in two days ago and threaten me." Her voice sailed out of a speaker beneath the glass. "He'd been given the sack for bullying, and his last wages hadn't been paid yet. He punched me in the stomach, so this little room was built."

"Why the fuck didn't the boss tell us?"

"I'm not sure. Do you want me to let him know you're here?"

"I should fucking say so."

She got on the phone, and a minute or so later, Mr Tadworth came through a doorway on the right in a dark-blue boilersuit.

"Uh, is everything okay?" Tadworth's usually ruddy face turned even redder at the sight of George and Greg, and he ran a hand through his sparse grey hair, then placed it on his tubby stomach.

"Err, does it look like it is?" Greg pointed to the receptionist's coffin. "Why weren't we informed about this?"

Tadworth tugged at the collar of his overalls. "I…um…I phoned the police so thought that would be enough. He was escorted from the building."

"He needs escorting from life or at the very least given a Cheshire," George snapped. "You pay us to protect you but didn't allow us to do that. This lady here was assaulted, and she deserves compensation and knowing the bloke's been dealt with properly. Who did it?"

"Terry Meeks."

George rolled his eyes. "That tosser. Right, in future, you ring us if someone ponces you or your staff about, got it?"

Tadworth nodded, fear in his eyes. "Sorry, I just assumed, with the police and everything…"

"You know what they say about assuming. Now to the reason we're here. Have you just taken on a bloke called Benedict Rufus Stallworth?"

Tadworth glanced to the receptionist.

She shook her head. "I've not heard that name, but a man signed a contract yesterday. He's taking over Terry's position. Let me just double-check what he's called." She tapped on her keyboard.

George stared at Tadworth. "Do you not have anything to do with the hiring side of things, then?"

"No, that would be the assistant manager."

George looked at a name plate on the counter. The receptionist's name was Paula Hobbs—he'd get some flowers sent to her, a nice box of chocolates. He whispered to Greg, "Can you go and get one of the compensation envelopes out of the glove box?"

Greg nodded and walked out.

Paula smiled. "Here we are. Reginald Noakes."

"Hang on." George sent that name to Mason and Flint along with the order to find out who he was, whether he'd lived in Manchester, and how often he had constipation—he wanted to know every-bloody-thing. "What did he look like?"

"Greyish beard and hair."

"Sounds like the man we're after. When does he start?"

"Tomorrow at eight in the morning. Said he didn't want any evening shifts."

I bet he fucking doesn't. "I doubt very much he'll turn up, but if we can't find him in the meantime and he comes in, give me a ring. We'd like a little word with him, but don't let on that we've been here."

Greg came back and handed George the envelope.

George gestured for Paula to slide the glass window across. He tossed the money through. "That's for any trauma you've suffered, and I apologise that one of our residents was a cock to you. If your *boss* had let us know about Terry"—George gave the tubby man an evil glare—"then you'd have been compensated sooner." He turned to Tadworth. "Do you need a refresher on the rules?"

"Um, no. I've got the gist."

"Good."

George strode out and got in the car. While waiting for Greg, he stared through the glass doors. His brother appeared to be giving Tadworth a dressing down.

George messaged Lil.

GG: YOU SAID GUV DIDN'T WANT TO MEET UP LAST NIGHT. HAVE YOU MADE CONTACT TODAY TO GET HIM TO THE RED LION LATER?

He worried she wouldn't be able to answer straight away if she was singing her lungs out at Elm House, but she pinged a reply back.

LIL: YES. SEVEN O'CLOCK.

GG: OKAY, SEE YOU SHORTLY AFTER THAT.

Greg slid in and put his seat belt on. "That Tadworth really boiled my piss more than usual for some reason."

"Perhaps because he didn't follow the rules?"

"More like he didn't think we were necessary because the police were involved. It doesn't fucking matter, we still need to be kept in the loop. With Freya, and now Paula being thumped, I keep thinking of our mum."

"Men punching women happens a lot more than we thought. What did you say to him?"

"That I'd chop his bollocks off if there was a repeat performance. I reminded him that all employees should be treated like family, and Paula didn't deserve for this to be swept under the carpet by the police."

George laughed. "A man after my own heart."

"Yeah, well, he got on my nellies."

George took a sweet out of the glove box, noting he needed to top up the money envelopes and buy a new bag of lemon sherbets. "Lil's meeting Guv at seven. Red Lion."

Greg nodded and reversed out of the space. "Unless we see him in the meantime, then that's a date to bring him in. We'll have to speak to Lil about the plan of action."

Their phone bleeped.

George picked it up. "It's Flint. I asked him and Mason to look into Reginald Noakes."

FLINT: THERE ARE A FEW OF THEM, BUT TWO STOOD OUT. ONE DIED IN LONDON, AGED FIFTY-THREE, ONE MONTH BEFORE ANOTHER NOAKES, WITH THE SAME DATE OF BIRTH, POPPED UP IN MANCHESTER.

"Fuck me." George read the message out to Greg. "Guv either got lucky with finding a man who'd died so he could nick his identity…"

"Or he killed him so he *could* nick it."

"Clever bastard."

Greg clutched the steering wheel tighter. "If he was the East End Stalker and is also the Coin Creep…"

George reckoned they sounded like they starred in a episode of *Scooby Doo,* but he answered anyway. "Then he's definitely the one who's bothering Avery. He got rid of Pax because he might have been caught by him. Too much of a coincidence?"

"Life's full of them, bruv, you know that."

"Seems it's full of tosser men an' all. Come on, let's pay Terry Meeks a visit. I feel another Cheshire coming on."

Chapter Twenty

Approaching forty and feeling older than that, Terry sat on the sofa scratching his balls. His wife, Willow, had gone mad at him when he'd lost his job, but if she knew why, she wouldn't have clouted him on the arm with her new Tefal frying pan—which, she'd said, was bloody fantastic because it was truly non-stick.

Terry couldn't bear to tell her he'd got the sack for 'bullying', but there'd been a valid reason for it, one that would break her heart.

And he was going to have to break it. He couldn't do this on his own anymore.

"Bullying, my arse." It was a lame term anyway. What he'd actually done was grip up a bloke who deserved everyone knowing who he was. Of course, Cod, old Halibut's cousin, had denied Terry's accusations, but…

"I know what I saw, and no one can tell me otherwise. Fucking oxygen thief, he is."

Terry sighed. He was meant to be doing some housework, but the loss of his job, which he'd had since he'd left school, had hit him hard. He'd hit Paula hard, too, wished he could take that back, and that was *another* thing he hadn't told the wife. The police had let him off with a caution, considering they knew exactly who and what Cod was, but what if Paula changed her mind and decided to press charges for assault? What then? And how long would it be before the gossip-vine piped up and Willow found out anyway?

Add that to the secret he'd been keeping, and he was a tad depressed. Helpless.

The doorbell rang, and he jumped up to go to the door. Willow had ordered the weekly online shop to be delivered during the day instead of the usual evening slot, seeing as he was 'sitting at home on his lazy arse' now. He didn't mind putting it away, it meant he got first dibs on the chocolate Hobnobs and the salt and vinegar Discos.

He opened the door, bracing himself to unload the shopping from the green crates, hoping Willow had remembered to click the 'bag' box, otherwise the job would be harder than it needed to be. One thing he couldn't abide was trying to get each individual item out of the crates while the delivery bloke stood there watching. It was too much pressure, same as when he couldn't get his stuff in carrier bags quickly enough at the checkout.

Before he had a chance to register who stood there, a fist popped out and landed on his forehead. He staggered back, bashing into the cupboard under the stairs, the knob digging into his hip. Jesus, his eyes watered.

So Cod had sent one of his nephews round to sort him out, had he?

He blinked, vision fuzzy. Two shapes came inside and shut the door. Fuck, was he seeing double? That knock to the head must have been harder than he'd thought.

"Listen to me," Terry said. "You can tell that fishy cunt he can send you here to hit me all he likes, he's still a paedo."

"What?" a man said.

Oh Jesus. Oh, fuck me sideways.

Terry strained to see…

George and Greg.

"Fishy cunt?" George asked. "Paedo?"

"Cod." Terry stumbled to sit on the stairs and rubbed his forehead. "Fucking Nora, I bet I've got a right bruise."

"I'll give you more than a bruise in a minute. Paedo. Elaborate."

Terry didn't trust these two. They smiled sometimes when going after people, making them think they were mates, then wallop, you were on your arse. Seemed they'd bypassed the smiling stage for him, unless he just hadn't seen any grins.

Terry narrowed his eyes. "Why are you here first?"

George sighed. "That isn't how this works normally, but you've piqued my interest, so I'm willing to let you have your say before I do anything drastic. We're here because you bullied someone at work and punched Paula. Ring any bells?"

"As a matter of fact, I've done nothing but think about it since it happened. I sent Paula some flowers this morning with an apology on the card. The poor cow didn't deserve me getting arsey, but she wouldn't listen about Cod when I went to pick up my wages—which weren't even bloody ready."

"I assume you mean Cod the bloke, not the actual fish."

"Yeah. Halibut's cousin. You know, that old fella with the gammy leg and lazy eye."

"What about him? You'd better give me an answer pretty sharpish, otherwise I'll do what I came here to do."

"What's that?"

"Give you a Cheshire."

"Nah, nah…" Terry shook his head. Regretted it. Pain throbbed. "It isn't me you ought to be cutting."

George stepped closer and bent down, getting in Terry's face. "Why don't you hurry the fuck up and tell me then, because my patience is wearing thinner than a tart's thong."

"Can we… I need a fag. Back garden? Willow won't let me smoke indoors."

"Depends whether any of your neighbours will overhear our conversation."

"Nah, both sides are at work." Terry got up and shuffled down the hallway into the kitchen, an even worse headache coming on. He waited for another bash to his nut from behind, but it never came. "Help yourself to coffee. It's fresh in the pot." Well, about half an hour old, but whatever.

George glanced at the machine. "Don't mind if we do."

Greg went to a cupboard in search of cups.

Terry opened the back door and took a scratched and battered baccy tin from his hoody pocket that used to belong to his dad. He'd spent a fair while making rollies this morning to pass some time, so he lit one and popped the tin away.

George walked over and folded his arms. "Let's have it, then."

Terry shuddered at the memory, the awful things he'd seen. He took a deep breath. "Bear with me, because this is painful. Right, my kid's been acting funny lately, you know, secretive an' that. A while back when she was asleep, I took her laptop and had a look at her browsing history. Now, Summer, that's my daughter, she told me and Willow she visited this site that was a safe space to talk, there were no private messages, but she *lied* to us. I had a look, and there's this 'kid' talking to her in a separate chat box rather than the open forum."

"Why say 'kid' in air quotes?"

"Because I don't think it's a kid. The username was Fishy_For_Life. Anyway, I didn't think of Cod at first because the conversation included bits about Fishy going to lakes with his dad and grandad. He seemed to know a lot about maggots and reels and shit, so as I say, I didn't think anything. Plus I go fishing. Summer used to come with me when she was little, so I thought she just had something in common with a lad. Her username is Mermaid, see. So I scrolled down over a period of weeks, and it got a bit more serious."

"How d'you mean?"

"Summer sent him photos—Fishy kept badgering her for ones without makeup. Then they progressed to *other* ones." Terry couldn't unsee them, and it felt wrong to keep having them pop up in his head when he was trying to fall asleep at night. "She was naked."

George reared his head back in shock as Greg brought coffees over and put them on the dining table.

"What's the site?" George asked, his jaw muscles spasming.

"London Teens. There's this forum with loads of topics, shit like favourite popstars, hobbies, that kind of thing. All the kids chat on it. A bit like Reddit."

"Remind us how old Summer is." Greg sat and leaned his forearms on the table.

"Thirteen." Terry took a massive drag of his rollie, but the fucking thing had gone out. He lit it again and inhaled. Blew the smoke out. "As you can imagine, I was disgusted she'd been roped into doing that—coerced more like, going by what Fishy had said—and I felt sorry for her that she'd thought she had to do it because…" He scrunched his eyes closed. Opened them to find the twins staring at him.

George picked up a cup and sipped. "Because…?"

"A while after she'd sent a load of rude images, different poses and whatever—he'd specified what he wanted—Fishy told her if she didn't give him money, he'd come after me and Willow. He asked her for twenty quid, and if she didn't give it to him, he'd also tell her mates she was a slag and spread her pictures around social media. It came out of the blue, know what I mean? Like, they'd been getting on fine, she even called him her *boyfriend* in the chat, then that happened. First of all he told her to put the cash in a coloured envelope and leave it in a bin outside Home Bargains in town. He wanted her to do it every week for a month, then he'd 'let her go'. The other times were different bins in different places."

"What did you do?"

"Would *could* I do? By the time I'd read what was going on, the end of the month for her to deliver the last payment had come and gone. He stopped talking to her. She hasn't been right since. Moody, stays in her room most of the time."

"I assume she has her own money?"

"Yeah, she works some evenings down the chippy. She told Fishy this, so I've been giving her a lift there and picking her up in case he gets it into his head to turn up. She thought that was odd, seeing as the chippy is only a couple of streets away from here, but I didn't want to give the perv a chance to get hold of her. I made some bullshit excuse up about it being dark and there being so much knife crime, it isn't safe. She gets the bus to and from school with a mate who calls for her, so I wasn't worried there."

"Have you approached her about it?"

"I wanted to, but I violated her privacy and she'd never trust me again, so I decided to find out who the fucker was. I went on London Teens, didn't I, made up a username, and tried to find Fishy. He wasn't on there—not a single fish-related name apart from Summer's Mermaid. Anyway, the other day when I got the sack, I'd gone to work in a right old mood because I was trying to find a way to tell Willow what had gone on; she'd know how to approach Summer, she's good with stuff like that." Terry relit his rollie again and inhaled. "It was break time, and the canteen was packed apart from a seat next to Cod."

"Right…"

"So I sat by him and happened to glance over at his phone."

"I know what's coming," George said.

"Yeah, he was on London Teens in a private chat as Market_Boy. *Boy*, not man, and a creepy old one at that."

"So he works at the factory *and* on the market?"

"He's only on the market Saturdays to give Halibut's son a break. Jason took over after his dad died and put Cod out to pasture for the most part. Cod's now part-time at the factory to top up his pension."

"So what happened next in the canteen?"

"I saw red. I mean, I know *I* went on that site, but that was to find the cunt who'd groomed my daughter, but what the fuck was *Cod* doing on there? I scraped my chair back and gripped the fucker up, pinning him down on the table, food flying, the lot. I asked him what he was playing at, noncing on kids, and he started laughing. I swear to God, if I see him on his own in the dark, he's a goner."

"Don't worry about that. Go on."

"Before I could beat the shit out of him, Tadworth comes stalking in, the twat, and breaks us apart. He wouldn't listen to a word I said, so I shouted that Cod was a paedo so people could at least keep an eye on him if they saw him near their kids. I got my marching orders, then there was that issue with Paula."

"What the hell did you hit her for? Granted, I get you'd be in a state, because what you've been through is bloody hard, but seriously? Hitting a woman?"

"I lost my rag, took it out on her. She didn't have my wages ready, hadn't sent it out on the system, and I needed it so I could pay someone to look into the site. Lay a trap for whoever Fishy is—you can bet he's changed his name and is prowling again. I can't let another girl go through that."

"Why didn't you just put a post up in the forum, outing the bloke? Warning other girls?"

"Because I wanted to catch him red-handed."

George tutted. "Right, that could take months, and that's better than protecting the girls sooner, is it? Or, I don't know, you could have let us deal with it, or contacted the site owners, the police."

Terry hung his head—George's sarcasm had clearly hurt. "I wasn't thinking straight."

"No, you weren't. We'll get a couple of people on this, get the site closed down so they can do an investigation."

Terry nodded. Finally finished his rollie. "What about Summer?"

"You grow some balls and become the parent not the friend—*she's* not in charge of how things go in this house, you are. You tell her you looked at her shit because you were worried. For all you know, she could be dying to tell you and her mum but can't bring herself to."

Terry flicked his rollie away, came in and shut the door.

The doorbell rang again.

"Fuck me, that'll be the Asda shop. Can you give me a minute?"

George shook his head. "Park your arse. Greg will deal with the delivery man."

Terry sat at the table. "Am I still getting a Cheshire? You know, for Paula?"

"No, we've sorted that issue with a bit of cash, but I'm warning you, if we find out you've clocked a woman again..."

"I won't, I swear. I'm a prick but not a woman beater. That was a one-off. You can ask Willow. I've never laid a hand on her." Terry rubbed his eyes. "I need to find a new job. It's not like Tadworth will take me back, is it."

George took his phone out. He typed on the screen, presumably sorting someone to look into London Teens. With the pressure off, Terry let the stinging tears fall.

Greg walked in with about five bags hanging off each hand. George glanced at his brother. They seemed to speak without words, and it gave Terry the willies.

Greg nodded.

George smiled. "You've got yourself a new job."

Terry frowned, his heart beating fast. "Eh?"

"Martin could do with a hand collecting protection money—as in you going round with him. You're a big bloke, and he's not. You'd be his bodyguard. Are you up for it?"

Terry's world brightened a tad. "Yep."

Greg looked at George again. "Fancy a piece of Cod, bruv?"

Chapter Twenty-One

When the news came that a woman's body had been found in a house in Princeton Avenue, Lil wanted to be sick. Had Ron lied to her about Guv not having a job on last night? Was the intended target the woman, not a man? Or had Guv *lied? Confused, she couldn't get her thoughts into any coherent order. She was consumed by being bullshitted by either man, and the fridge thing, Guv moving the contents, it pointed to him being sinister as fuck.*

Mum was having a nap, and Guv was out getting some shopping in, so it gave Lil time to reread the article in the local newspaper which they had delivered daily. She'd been too busy to have a sit-down and browse it earlier—she'd done the housework then sat and watched a bit of telly with Mum.

WOMAN FOUND DEAD!

THE EAST END STALKER HAS STRUCK AGAIN!

Lacey Kopp, 22, was discovered at her home in Princeton Avenue this morning by her sister, Judy. Lacey had been strangled in her bed. A police source has revealed that items were moved in typical Stalker fashion, confirmed by Judy, and the signature, three coins left on the hallway floor, was present. There is no further news at this time, but if you saw or heard anything in Princeton Avenue last night, or in the surrounding areas, please contact the police.

Shit. What if she'd been seen? What if someone had recognised her and reported her? She'd have to say she'd been following Guv. She wasn't about to take any blame, and if it meant the police rounded him up based on her statement, so be it. And another thing—Christ, she could get in trouble for not phoning the coppers now. She'd seen Guv in Princeton Avenue, and any normal woman would let the Old Bill know once they'd read that article.

Lil contemplated everything. What if he'd gone in there to kill the man, had found only the woman, and left? Someone else, the Stalker, could then have gone inside. Maybe Guv hadn't locked the back door, giving the other fella easy access.

"Stop trying to make this fit what you want it to be, you silly cow," she muttered.

"Talking to yourself is the first sign of madness."

Lil's head shot up, her heart pounding. Guv stood in the kitchen doorway—she hadn't heard him coming in—several bags of shopping in each hand. She laughed to cover her unease, praying he hadn't caught what she'd said. She quickly swept through her options, coming to the conclusion she'd pretend everything was fine. If he was the Stalker, she'd fucking kill him. She had ample opportunity, but then again, suspicion might fall on her, seeing as they were a couple and Guv lived here. The partner was always suspected, weren't they.

She was going to have to tell Ron. They could deal with Guv at the cottage.

"What were you on about anyway?" Guv came in and put the bags on the worktop next to the sink, getting on with emptying them.

"Just moaning to myself. A washing machine has broken at the laundrette, and I need to get someone in to fix it."

As his back was to her, she relaxed a little—she wouldn't have to concentrate on schooling her features. But she had a thought. She couldn't speak to him without seeing his *face, she had to gauge whether he was lying to her, so she got up and joined him in emptying the bags.*

"Did you get your job done last night?" she asked.

"Yeah. There's no fly in the ointment anymore." A muscle in his jaw flickered.

"Are you allowed to tell me who it was and what he did?" She took a four-pack of baked beans out and put them on the draining board.

"The usual, scum dealing drugs without permission."

She rested her hand on a packet of frozen sausages, the chill seeping through her skin. "Sounds to me like Ron hasn't got the Estate wrapped up as well as it should be. He must be slacking if all these men are able to deal on Cardigan. I mean, those jobs you're doing, they're all for the same thing."

Guv paused in removing a string bag of onions. "Hmm, I hadn't realised you were keeping tabs—again."

She shrugged. "Things like that stand out to me, that's all, and you know I'm like a dog with a bone. The last few jobs especially have been drug dealers, so…"

"They're like ants. You get rid of one nest and another one sprouts up. But you're right, Ron needs to get a better handle on it, not that I'd tell him that. I just do as I'm told."

They got on with putting things away, then Lil stuck the kettle on and made tea. At the table, Guv sitting opposite, she poked a finger at the news article.

"Have you heard about this?"

He glanced at her finger. "What's that, then?"

"The Stalker's been at it again. Some poor cow copped it in Princeton Avenue."

Guv's face drained of colour, but he recovered quickly. "That bloke's been around for a long time. Makes you wonder whether he'll ever get caught."

"He'll slip up at some point, they always do."

Guv picked up his cup and stared past her into the garden. "Nah, he seems too clever to me."

"I wonder what the coins mean. It's so specific."

"Fuck knows."

They drank in silence, Lil watching him. He was uneasy, his eyes flicking all over the place, and his hands shook, sloshing his tea about. The radio came on in the living room, so Mum must have woken up. Lil hoped she didn't come in here. If Guv was riled up enough, he might show a side of himself Lil would hate to see.

She ploughed on. "Whoever he is, well, Ron will find out eventually. Maybe he'll send someone to kill him now Bod's dead. You're obviously the drug-dealer killer these days, so you won't be asked—"

"Give it a rest, Lil."

"Give what a rest?"

"You've made your point, I've been demoted to sorting the lowlifes. Did you ever stop to think what you're saying is emasculating? Like, you're basically saying I'm not good enough for the bigger jobs."

"I didn't realise me making a correct observation was emasculating, but I apologise if I made you feel that way. But maybe you've *got the problem—it's obviously bothering you that Ron doesn't trust you with the meaty stuff anymore. Talk to him, say you're unhappy bumping off all the dregs."*

"I might well do that."

She changed tack. "I'm a bit worried, to be honest."

"What about?"

"There was that attempted robbery at the laundrette last night, and when I get home, you're always out. Me and Mum are sitting ducks, because with that woman being killed in Princeton Avenue, well, it's a bit too close to home, isn't it? What if he comes after us?"

"Why would he? He's called Stalker for a reason. He obviously watches his targets and makes sure they live alone. And he doesn't kill all of them, remember. Those who've reported that they think they're being watched and stuff was moved in their houses are still alive. He's left them alone because it's too dangerous to keep watching them."

That last sentence had come out sounding like a fact.

"Weird that he rearranges what's in the fridge, though," she continued. "There's got to be a reason for that an' all. Actually, do you remember you did that here when you first moved in? Said you couldn't find anything if it wasn't in order?" She was pushing it and sensed he was trying hard not to blow, but as far as he knew, she was chatting the breeze like she usually did. It wasn't her fault if he was the Stalker and he didn't like discussing it. Or her probing, as he'd see it.

"He'll have his reasons."

All the answers he'd given were reasonable, the sort of thing said by an innocent man. If it wasn't for her seeing him go inside that house and Ron saying Guv hadn't had a job last night, she might have believed him. Of course, this could still be a misunderstanding on her part, but she didn't think so.

She laughed. "Lucky your job wasn't in Princeton Avenue, eh? It'd take some explaining if you were seen there. Ron wouldn't want you dropping him in the shit."

Guv narrowed his eyes at her. "I was nowhere near Princeton fucking Avenue."

"Blimey, no need to bite my head off."

Mum appeared in the doorway. "There's just been a thing on the radio. The Stalker's killed another woman."

Guv swallowed and gritted his teeth, his cheeks going red.

Lil played it casual. "Yeah, I read it in the paper. Poor cow."

Mum came and sat at the table. "He cocked up this time."

Guv's head whipped round to face her. "What?"

"Someone saw him standing in the victim's back garden. They took a picture of him, but the flash didn't go off. But someone might recognise his shape, don't you think?"

Lil patted Mum's hand. "He'll get caught soon, you mark my words."

Guv scooted his chair back and stood. "I'm going out."

"Can you pop to the little Co-op on your way back," Lil asked. "I noticed you didn't pick up any strawberries *earlier." She waited for his reaction to her stressing that word, the moment when the memory of him eating a strawberry in Princeton Avenue hit home.*

He scowled. "So sorry, m'lady, I'll remember to do that for you."

The acid in his tone and the implication Lil thought she was queen of the castle had Mum's eyebrows shooting up.

"No need to be sarky," Lil said. "It was your turn to do the shopping this week. It's not like I don't do my share."

Guv's shoulders slumped. "Again, I'm sorry. Didn't mean to snap."

"You seem tense," Mum said. "Is that bloody Ron expecting too much of you?"

Guv walked to the front door. "It's nothing to do with Ron."

He left, and Lil gave her mother a smile to say she wasn't hurt by Guv's behaviour. The last thing she wanted was her worrying about shit she didn't need to.

"Poor man, he's so stressed." Mum sighed.

"Want a cuppa?"

"Please."

Lil got up and re-boiled the kettle. "What do you fancy for dinner? Guv picked up some fish that looks nice. Got it from Halibut."

"It's handy you've got a bloke who's pally with the fish man."

That gave Lil pause. Maybe she should go and speak to Halibut, see what he had to say, but she risked him telling Guv she'd been asking questions, and she didn't want him to know she was onto him. If she'd even got this right. It annoyed her, how all the facts were there, right in front of her, but a little part of her persisted in trying to see Guv in a good light. It was because he'd been so nice to her and Mum, and she cared about him a lot, thinking she'd finally found the right man for her. She almost wished her first instincts had been right and he was having an affair. It would be so much easier to deal with than this.

She squeezed a teabag against a cup and made up her mind. She was going to tell Ron later. He could string Guv up in the steel room and torture the truth out of him. Even if Guv only admitted to going into that house for other reasons and it meant he wasn't the Stalker, she could cope with it.

Guv came home in time for dinner. Lil had asked one of her employees to cover her tonight. She'd get hold of Ron and meet him at the cottage to tell him everything, then he could do what had to be done. Lil had battered and fried the fish, peeling and cutting up the potatoes instead of being lazy and nipping down the chippy like she usually would. They all sat round the table, Guv jittery but quiet, and she swore he had tears in his eyes at one point.

"Are you okay, love?" Mum asked him.

Guv nodded. "Yeah."

"You don't seem it."

Lil waited for him to bark at Mum—if he did, she wouldn't stand for it, and he knew it. She'd toss him out on his fucking ear.

"Nothing a break from London won't cure."

"Oh, how lovely. Are you planning a holiday?" Mum ate a chunk of fish.

"Something like that."

"I did wonder when the post came last week. It looked like you got something from the passport office."

Lil hid her shock. Was he planning to skip the country?

"I'll be fine here," Mum said, "so no thinking you have to take me with you and Lil."

"It doesn't seem like I'm going with him. This is the first I've heard of a break, and I don't even have a passport," Lil said.

Guv ignored that jibe and smiled at Mum, placing a hand on her shoulder. "You're a good woman."

Mum seemed chuffed. "I try to be, although if you knew me years ago, you might not think that."

Lil recalled what Ron had said, and anger brewed. "What you were in the past isn't who you are now. We're all entitled to make mistakes when we're young, and you're no different. We're growing all the time, and we can change, make sure we don't repeat what we've done before." She stared at Guv pointedly. "If we stop doing shit that means we're bad, then it shows we're trying to make amends."

"True," Mum said.

Guv pushed pieces of fish around his plate. "Sorry, but I'm not really hungry."

Lil shrugged. "It's all right. Next door's cat will be happy. Pippy likes cod. I'll just pick the batter off before I take it round."

Guv got up and walked out, saying over his shoulder, "I've got another job on tonight. It's a long one, so I'll be sleeping in the car."

My Mini. *Now she couldn't go to the cottage. She couldn't get a cab because it would leave a trail as to where she'd been, and she wasn't going to walk all that way. She'd have to get Ron to pick her up in one of his disguises. "Nice of you to ask if you can use it."*

He paused in the hallway. "Can I?"

"Yes, but like I've told you before, I'm not happy about it. Ron should be giving you a stolen one."

He walked off, up the stairs.

Mum pursed her lips. "You could get into trouble if he's caught doing whatever and your car's involved."

Lil shrugged. "I'll say he took it without asking."

"Good. I don't want you being like I was and covering up for a bloke. It only leads to heartache and guilt."

Now, more than ever, Lil thought Ron's lie had a grain of truth to it. Maybe he had *slept with Mum, or he at least had something on her regarding the men she'd been with. But like Lil had said, that was in the past. And anyway, whatever her mother had done, she would love her no matter what.*

Guv had left with a holdall, so Lil snooped in the bedroom. Yes, his bag could contain a change of clothes and a blanket because he was supposedly sleeping in the car, but she wasn't stupid and no longer wanted to kid herself that he was a top bloke.

She opened the wardrobe, but not many clothes were missing, his two drawers revealing much the same. The ones she couldn't see were probably in the wash.

So he hadn't left her, then.

"Yet..." a nasty little voice whispered.

His nightstand held a passport and birth certificate, and she opened them. Shock powered through her. The birth certificate was for Reginald Noakes, and the passport photo was Guv but with a beard, but again, it was in Reginald's name. She thought back to a month or so ago, when Guv had said he was too tired to shave. He'd lied. He'd grown the fucking beard so he could get this picture taken, then shaved it off again. Such a deceitful little bastard.

He hadn't killed Reginald for Ron, so he must have done it for himself so he could steal his identity. Had he been so spooked by today's news and what he'd have seen as a grilling from Lil that he'd scarpered, forgetting to take the passport and certificate with him? It didn't make sense why he'd leave them here otherwise.

She found her phone on the bed and, shaking, picked it up to message Ron. But she stopped herself. She wanted to confront Guv on this when he came back tomorrow—and he would, because if he was planning on fucking off, if he'd ordered that passport, then he'd need it.

When he got home, she'd be waiting.

Lil opened her eyes to bright sunlight seeping around the edges of the bedroom curtains and the bedside clock informing her it was just past nine. She'd fallen asleep in her clothes on top of the covers. A glance across at Guv's side showed a smooth quilt, so he hadn't been home. She launched out of bed and pulled the drawer of his nightstand open.

The passport and birth certificate were gone.

"That bastard came back and got it," she muttered and shivered at the thought of him creeping into the bedroom, her not waking up, yet usually he clattered about. Was that how it had been with those women, all stealthy silence? They hadn't heard him, and by the

time they'd realised he was in their house, he'd had his hands around their throats?

This time, she messaged Ron.

LIL: I THINK HE'S LEFT ME.

RON: IT'S BETTER THIS WAY.

He's fucking got rid of him.

Lil digested that. Decided she was okay with it. Ron may well have cottoned on that Guv was the Stalker, or because Lil had queried one of his jobs, plus asked about Reginald, Ron had realised Guv was up to something and he'd dealt with it accordingly. Still, she'd probe for more. An outright admittance.

LIL: WHAT DO YOU MEAN?

RON: THINK ABOUT IT. HE'S NOT WORTH SHIT IF HE CAN JUST UP AND LEAVE. YOU DESERVE BETTER THAN THAT.

LIL: I'M NEVER TRUSTING A MAN AGAIN.

RON: NOT EVEN ME?

LIL: ESPECIALLY NOT YOU.

She sat with her tears, letting the hurt take over, but only for a little while. This was the last time she'd cry over a bloke, and maybe this was what she deserved. Noelle thought Bod had fucked off without a word, and Lil was going through the same thing. Karma had paid her a visit, but from now on she'd be like Mum, doing better, stuffing her past into a box and wiping the slate clean.

She'd become a new woman. Hard of heart in some respects, yes, and definitely not taking any shit, but she'd help others, be kinder, redeeming herself. Maybe then she could forgive herself for everything she'd done.

But she doubted it.

Chapter Twenty-Two

The twins had gone home, put forensic suits on, and got in the van. Today's logo on the sides was a fish on the end of a line, exactly what Cod was going to be—caught on their hook, no escaping. Mason had done some snooping, and the results weren't pretty. George was steaming angry, fit to fucking burst. At least the news had come back clear on Mr Goode, so that was one less worry. Freya would likely be fine with him.

"There's something about killing an old man that feels wrong," George said in the passenger seat, "but like you taught me with women, all people can be bastards, their gender or age doesn't give them a pass."

Greg pulled up in the factory cark park, close to the building, and nodded to their cleaning crew in an SUV ahead, waiting for their cue. "Nope. Think of it this way. Cod is old, yes, but that means he could have been noncing for *years*."

George inhaled deeply, his rage mounting. His Mad side had been knocking to take over ever since Mason's message had come through. "All those kids…and they've probably kept quiet even as adults."

"I know."

They left the vehicle and strode inside.

Paula looked up and did a double-take. That'd be the white suits, then. "Oh, back so soon?"

George smiled. "We've had a word with Terry. What he did is inexcusable, but if it makes you feel better, his anger wasn't directed specifically at you. You were in the wrong place at the wrong time—you could have been a bloke and he'd have still lashed out. He has a hell of a lot on his plate, and ordinarily he'd never have touched you. He's very sorry."

"Well, yes, that does make me feel better, actually. He's always been nice to me in the past, so I was more upset that it was *me* he punched."

"What was he saying about Cod when he came to collect his wages?"

"That he's a paedo. No one believes that, of course. Cod is too sweet to be doing anything like that."

"Is he still here?"

"Yes, he finishes at four-thirty."

"Can you page him or whatever it is you do?"

She seemed uncomfortable. "I should talk to Mr Tadworth first..."

George reined his temper in. "Yeah, you do that. Tell him The Brothers want a word with Cod and there's no choice in the matter."

Paula got on the phone and relayed the message, then peered at them through the glass partition. "He'll go and get him." She paused. "Did you...did you hurt Terry?"

"No. Do you want us to?"

"No, violence never solves anything."

George grinned. "It solves a lot of things, love."

Paula dipped her head and got on with some work. Greg rolled his eyes at George regarding Paula's comment. She was clearly in the forgiveness camp. Nice of her, but nah, violence was the only way to go in this case.

They stood waiting for about three minutes. Eventually, Cod appeared in the doorway, shuffling through on his gammy leg, one eye looking at George, the other off having a party by itself. In other circumstances George would have felt sorry for him and nosed into helping the old boy get on the waiting list for an operation to straighten it, but this wasn't other circumstances, so he didn't give a shit about the man's lazy eye.

"Have you come about Terry and what he said?" Cod asked from the doorway. "He called me a paedophile, a pervert, and a nonce."

"Yeah, we've come about that." Greg walked over to him just as Tadworth appeared behind Cod. "Come over here a second."

Greg guided the old man to the middle of the reception area.

George gestured for Tadworth to come farther in. "Don't let anyone else past that door." He stared at Cod. "What were you doing on London Teens?"

Tadworth appeared confused, his eyebrows beetling. "What on earth's that?"

"A place for teenagers to chat. A place that will hopefully be closed down shortly." George glared at the old man.

Cod's face flushed. "I don't know what you're talking about."

"I think you do. Those names Terry called you, they're right on the money, aren't they."

"*What*? I'm not a kiddie fiddler!"

"I beg to differ, sunshine." George took his phone out—or Mad did—and read Mason's message. "Nineteen ninety-eight, imprisoned for three years for indecent exposure to a five-year-old girl. Twenty twelve, imprisoned for six years and placed on the sex offenders' register for taking photos of little girls at the swimming pool where you watched them from the canteen, plus having indecent pictures of minors on your computer, plus sexual assault on a minor. After you got out, you didn't get caught, but I bet you've still been at it, haven't you. Before, too."

"That's all lies. I didn't do it. They got the wrong man."

"Who was it, then?"

"Halibut!"

"Blaming a dead fella is a bit rank." George glanced at Paula. "Take yourself off somewhere, love, and don't come back for two hours. Get your hair done or something, not that I'm saying it needs it."

Tadworth, clearly trying to digest what had been said, blustered, "Now hang on a minute…"

Mad stared at him. "Are you seriously going to tell me, considering what we're dealing with here, that your receptionist has to sit there and watch me slit this bloke's bastard throat?"

Tadworth held his hands up. "Oh God, I don't want any trouble."

"There won't be any if you keep your mouth shut."

"But the police…"

"Who's going to tell them?"

Cod tried to get to the exit, but his dodgy leg hampered his progress. He got within two steps of it, then Greg gripped him by the back of his shirt collar and spun him round to face George who whipped his knife out. Paula left her cubicle, the door inside it slamming then locking, and

Tadworth fucked about with his boilersuit collar again.

Mad addressed Cod. "We don't tolerate people like you. The scourge of the fucking earth, the lot of you."

He sliced the man's neck, Tadworth's shriek getting louder with every sheet of blood that coasted down the front of Cod's shirt.

"Shut up," George said to Tadworth—Mad had gone, quickly retreating. "Now then, as a favour to you for letting us do this here, you can miss two months of protection money. Can't say fairer than that, can I?"

Tadworth heaved, a hand to his chest. "The blood, all that blood… The smell…"

George smiled. "Don't worry your little bobbing head about it." He jerked his thumb towards the glass front door where people waited to come in. "Our cleaning crew's going to make it all nice and tidy. As for us, we're taking the rubbish out, and you look like you could do with a cuppa. Off you sod, mate. And lock that door while you're at it."

Tadworth turned tail and ran the way he'd come, the door thudding closed, a *clunk* where he'd secured it.

Greg, still holding Cod upright, cocked his head. "I thought you'd have tortured this prick a bit first."

"The sooner men like him are gone, the better." George bent to pick up Cod's ankles. "Come on, let's feed the fish to the fishes."

Chapter Twenty-Three

Lil opted for a shiny black PVC catsuit tonight, easier to wipe blood off it. She hadn't bothered with a wig, instead wrapping her thinning hair in a colourful scarf. Minus the fruit on top, she resembled an older Carmen Miranda. Makeup the same as usual—she wouldn't be seen dead in public without any on—she stepped outside in her ballerina flats and leather coat, her handbag strap draped over her inner elbow.

In the cab, no sooner had she got comfortable than they'd arrived, the driver thanking her for the generous tip. She smiled at him then got out, scanning the street for a taxi. She clocked a white van, a logo on the side of a fish. She walked closer. Two men sat inside, big bastards, one with a ginger beard and hair, the other blond, his beard long.

The window wound down, and Ginger poked his head out. "All right, Lil?"

"George? Fuck me, I wouldn't have recognised you unless you'd spoken." It reminded her of when Guv had walked into the laundrette the other day. She really ought to get contact lenses so she could study people better when she didn't have her glasses on. "I thought you said you were going to use a black cab?"

"Changed our minds. We risked too many people thinking we were for hire. He's already in the pub by the way."

"Okay. Give me ten minutes to get him to come outside, all right?"

"Fine. You weren't wrong. It's looking like he's the East End Stalker. The same shit's been going on in Manchester all this time, only he's known as the Coin Creep up there."

"The what?"

"It'll become clear later. We reckon he's picked a new one out already, woman called Avery. We'll reveal everything once we've carted him off. Remember what we discussed. You know what you've got to do." He handed her an envelope.

She popped it in her bag. "Yep, I'm not thick. See you shortly."

Thankful she hadn't been stark raving bonkers in suspecting Guv, she pushed the door open and walked inside. The usual crowd were in tonight, plus a few more, and she nodded and waved to acknowledge their greetings. Some Saturday nights she still belted out songs here, so she was a bit of a star. It was the only claim to fame she had other than at Elm House, having given up doing her regular gigs ten years ago. Her dreams of making it as a professional singer had died a death.

"Thank you, thank you verra much," she said in her best Elvis impression. She checked where Guv was, gave him a brief smile, and made a drinking motion with her gloved hand to see if he wanted another pint, seeing as he only had an inch left in his glass. At his nod, she walked up to the bar and winked at Dave. "A vodka and tonic plus whatever that fella over there's having."

Dave glanced across at Guv. "Pint of bitter."

He'll be bitter all right once George has laid into him. "And one for your tab, of course."

"You're too good to me, Lil."

"Got to look after my favourite landlord, haven't I."

Dave seemed suspicious. "What are you after?"

"I'll tell you in a minute. Let's act normal for a sec. He's probably watching."

"Who? That bloke? How's things going with him anyway?" Dave poured the pint. "I saw you getting along quite well the other night."

"Between you and me, he won't be coming back in here again." She lowered her voice. "Sod it, I may as well just get this over and done with. It's The Guv'nor."

"Fuck me, I'd never have known."

"Hmm, I didn't realise it was him at first, so you're not the only one."

Dave put the pint on the bar and reached back to get her shot of vodka. He took a tonic water from a fridge and cracked the lid off. Poured. "So why won't he be coming in again?"

"Let's just say The Brothers have got wind of something he's done."

"Oh. Shit."

"Indeed. Do you remember the East End Stalker? What am I on about, you must do."

"You're shitting me. Him?" Dave jerked his head slightly at Guv and added ice to her drink.

"I'm not. All that crap stopped when he left London."

Dave shook his head. "Blimey."

"He'll be leaving with me after these drinks."

"I don't think you should be going with him, love, not if he's dodgy."

"It's fine, the twins are waiting outside in a van. They want me to ask you to turn your CCTV off, the camera directly out the front, and erase the footage to before their van shows up. It's the one with a fish on the side."

"I'll do it in a minute, but it won't stop them being caught on the council cameras. We're in the fucking high street, Lil."

"That's all right, their mate's sorting it, Bennett someone or other. There'll be a convenient outage, footage lost, that kind of thing." She winked and held her phone to the card reader to pay. "Just give us fifteen minutes of blackout after me and him have walked out."

"Not a problem."

Lil took the envelope out of her bag and slid it across the bar. "From the twins."

Dave quickly put it in his pocket.

Lil picked up the drinks and tottered over to Guv who sat at the same table as before. With the first hurdle of her instructions over, she moved on to phase two. She sat, placed the drinks down, and plonked her bag between her feet.

"Not stopping long?" Guv asked.

"What d'you mean?"

"You've kept your coat and gloves on."

"Oh, yeah, I wondered if we could have a quick one here then go to my place. I've got plenty of booze at home."

"Fine by me."

"What have you been up to today? Anything interesting?"

"Visiting old haunts before I start work."

Old haunts? Like the places you killed women? "Oh, did the twins set you up, then?"

"Nah, I landed a job at the factory down by The Eagle."

"Lovely. How were things last night?"

He jolted, frowning. "What?"

"You said you were with the twins and George had done a Cheshire."

Guv relaxed. "Oh, that. Yeah, this bird who lives opposite me was getting a bit of gyp off her fella. I saw it through the window, so I went over and gave him a pasting. George took over afterwards. Drove him off somewhere in a van."

Fuck. I hope they haven't got the same logo on the side tonight. He'll twig. "Ruddy hell, that was nice of you to step in. You're a right old knight in shining armour, aren't you."

"Yeah, well, I didn't like seeing her being walloped, did I. It's not on."

"Do you always come to the aid of damsels in distress?"

"If they deserve it."

She cocked her head. "And if they don't?"

"Some women receive what's due."

"Like your ex?"

"No, I never hurt her. *She* was the one who hurt *me*." He frowned again. "What are you getting at?"

"Nothing."

"Sounds like you're fishing to me."

"Fishing for what? The only thing I've cast my line out for is you coming to mine and giving me a good seeing to in a bit." Nauseated by the very thought of that, she smiled, but it had been necessary to say it so it threw him off the scent.

He grinned. "Saucy mare."

"I can be more than saucy." She drank half of her vodka to hide her distaste. "I've learned a fair few tricks since you've been away."

"What, in the bedroom?"

"You're in for a big surprise, put it that way."

"Fucking hell, you were always a goer."

"I'll show you what you missed out on." *My razor biting into your face*. "Hurry up with that pint, for God's sake, I need to get you home." She tossed the rest of her vodka back to steady her nerves. Getting him out of the pub and to the back of the van meant she was going to have to kiss him, and she didn't want to. Best to get it over with quickly.

Guv took four more swallows then put the remainder of his pint down. "Come on, then."

They stood, and she put her bag strap over her arm and tucked her other through his. The sooner the twins got him into the van, the sooner she could get this fucker out of her life. She waved to customers as she passed, Dave nodding to her. She assumed he meant the camera was now switched off, the footage wiped. At the door, Guv went out, which pissed her off. She was an independent woman, but she liked a man who held it open, letting *her* go through first.

Another black mark.

She glanced at the van. The twins weren't in it, as planned, so she walked along beside Guv on the left-hand side of him then stopped. He stopped, too, and stared down at her, his back to the kerb.

"Thought you wanted to get home?" he said.

"I do, but give us a kiss." She stood on tiptoes, gripped his upper arms, and put her lips to his. Every part of her rebelled against it—he'd stalked and killed women, was a weirdo pervert, and she wanted to run away. She opened her eyes and looked up at him to keep his attention on her. Caught sight of the baseball bat swinging from the left behind him, cracking onto the side of his head.

Guv went down like a sack of shit, Lil jumping back to get out of his way, but she didn't move far enough. He landed on his knees, face-planting into her stomach. The contact had her retching.

She stared at George who laughed, Greg coming forward to hold Guv beneath the armpits and drag him to the van doors. George opened one, and Greg stuffed a groaning Guv inside.

"Are you riding shotgun with me or getting in the back with him?" Greg asked.

"I'll get in the back," Lil said. "I want to have a chat with him—if he's even compos mentis."

"I'll cable tie his wrists and ankles, then." Greg climbed in the back.

George stood swinging the bat by his side. "I wanted to keep hitting him, but we need a word first, get a few confessions."

Lil nodded.

Greg got out, and Lil got in, sitting on a wheel arch beside a large plastic storage box containing tools. Guv lay on his side, arms tied behind him. Blood dripped from his head down his temple, wriggling over the side of his nose. The back door slammed, then the two at the front, and they were off.

"What the fuck, Lil?" Guv slurred.

"Don't act innocent. You're in a whole world of shit, you arsehole."

"What's this? Revenge for me leaving?"

"It's so much more than that. You lied to me the whole time we were together. I had no clue who you were."

"What are you *on* about?"

The van swerved around a corner, and Lil pressed her feet to the floor to stop herself tipping sideways. She grabbed the toolbox with one hand to balance herself. "You know damn well what I'm on about." She'd been told not to mention the East End Stalker, or the Coin Creep, but by God, she found it hard to keep it to herself.

Don't let the cat out of the bag, not yet.

She smirked. "You'll see."

"Who the fuck hit me?"

"You seriously have to ask me that?"

"Jesus wept, what did you get *them* involved for? Christ, my head's killing me."

"*I'll* be killing *you* soon, so have a think about what you're going to say when we get to where we're going, because we have a lot of questions for you."

"About what?"

She shook her head. "Shut up. You make me sick."

He asked more questions, but she ignored him, looking out of the windscreen between the twins' heads. They'd left the housing estate and went down a road with warehouses on the right. Greg pulled over, and George got out to open an iron-pole gate. He then waited, and Greg drove through into a little car park. The sound of the gate clunking shut at the same time Greg applied the handbrake had Lil eager to get out, away from Guv. Being in such close confines had bothered her more than she'd thought it would.

"Where are we?" Guv asked.

The back door opened, and she clambered outside, breathing deeply. Her aversion to speaking to him had grown. How was she going to manage to ask him all the questions she had stacked up in her brain? Everything in her had gone stone-cold, solid granite walls building up. Was her mind protecting her from more hurt? Yes, because she knew damn well he was going to lie to her again, make out he wasn't the Stalker, give her another bullshit story about why he'd left London.

She walked to the warehouse door. George held it open for her—now *there* was a gentleman—and she pushed yet another door and entered a vast space. Took it all in to get her bearings. Everything was set up at the far end.

Two doors to the right, a table farther along, things on top. She couldn't see well enough to make them out. In the top-right corner, stacks of foldable chairs, as well as a wooden one, and a spiked metal contraption attached to the wall. To the left, a TV, a sofa in front of it. Why was it all so far away? So if anyone ran they'd get caught before they reached the door?

She walked forward, scenting bleach in the air, as though the place had been cleaned. Had someone been killed in here recently, or did it always smell like this? Footsteps behind her and a something-being-dragged sound had her turning. Greg manhandled Guv past Lil, and George jogged to the table. Lil followed and stood there while Greg used a knife to slice the cable ties.

"Get undressed," he said to Guv.

Lil moved away to perch her arse on the top ledge of the sofa back. She folded her arms, wanting to see these two in action against a man she'd once loved.

"W-what?" Guv said.

"I know you're not deaf." Greg glared at him. "Take. Off. Your. Fucking. Clothes. If you make us do it, you'll see a side to me not many people do. This is George's domain, he's the nutter, but I'm not averse to getting involved. Do it, *now*!"

Guv stripped, his face flaming. He dropped his clothes in a pile on the floor and covered his tackle with both hands.

"No need to hide it, no one's interested in your saggy knackers," Greg said. "Sit the fuck down."

Guv glanced back at a wooden chair and sat on it. George came over with a coil of rope.

"Hands by your sides," Greg ordered.

Guv complied until he spotted George and the rope. He bolted to his feet and legged it towards the door. George whipped a gun out, aimed, and fired. Guv screamed, a bloom of red appearing on his calf, and he staggered forward, landing in a heap.

Greg swaggered over there. "That wasn't a sensible thing to do." He snatched at Guv's hair and dragged him across the floor to the chair. "Get the fuck up and sit your arse down—and don't move. If I have to repeat myself, I swear to God, you'll regret it."

George waited for Guv to park his arse then leaned into his face. "Looks like Greg's got the right old hump about something, doesn't it? It's men like you, treating women as though they're a pile of dog shit. God fucking help you, sunshine."

Lil stared in awe. She'd never seen Greg take the dominant role, and the way George stared at Guv, she wouldn't want to get on the wrong side of him either. The bloke was mental.

She smiled, looking forward to what came next.

Chapter Twenty-Four

Guv could have kicked himself for forgetting the most important things—the passport and birth certificate. He'd been so rattled by thinking Lil was onto him that he'd rushed collecting some of his clothes. He had so many, he doubted she'd see he'd taken a few bits, just enough to get him through a week. He'd find a laundrette here in Manchester and do a wash every Saturday.

His venture back into the house had been fraught with tension. Creeping around it had felt so wrong, unlike when he did it in other places. That house had been his sanctuary, Lil his rudder, and her mum was a good sort, treating him like her son. He'd ruined the only good thing he'd ever had by stalking. His greed in following his desires had led to him an alien place where everyone was a stranger.

He'd worried about waking Lil, and seeing her asleep in her clothes, no covers on, told him she was really rattled. She'd have stewed, likely thinking of going out and trying to find him. If her mum hadn't said about a passport arriving, Lil would have been none the wiser that he'd planned to leg it.

He'd wanted to kiss her on the head before he'd left for the last time, whisper that he loved her, thank her for loving him, but he couldn't risk her waking. So he'd walked out, leaving her Mini outside and trudging the streets towards the bus station. Worrying one of Ron's lot would spot him, ask why he carried a holdall. Or that they'd been sent out to apprehend him because Lil had told the leader Guv was acting suss.

He wiped tears from his eyes and trudged yet again through unfamiliar streets that would soon become familiar, maybe a comfort, him knowing he was safe in his new identity. He'd withdrawn all the money from his account and closed it last month a week prior to killing Reginald. That still bothered him, a kill for the only purpose of securing Guv a ticket to a life undetected by anyone in London, but it had been necessary. He'd had a nasty feeling that his time as the Stalker in London was coming to an end, and when Lil's mum had mentioned him fucking up, being seen in that back garden, he'd panicked, bolted.

He'd paid for a bedsit in a crummy, run-down part of the city for now, planning to lie low until he found a job and established himself as a regular face in the local boozer. He'd hole up this week, though, waiting for a beard to show its prickly face. Reginald had a beard, and it had given Guv the idea to hide himself behind one. Probably stupid of him to have had the passport and birth certificate sent to Lil's, but he hadn't had much choice.

Good job he'd grilled Reginald on whether he had a passport already, which he hadn't, so applying for one wouldn't have brought up any red flags. He'd got the place he'd been born out of him an' all so he could apply for a copy of the birth certificate. He'd hated himself at the time, still did, because the poor fucker had babbled about having kids and please, please don't kill me.

But Guv had killed him.

With thousands of pounds he'd earned from Ron stored in his backpack, which he'd carry around with him until he got the balls up to apply for a bank account in Reginald's name, Guv didn't have to worry about where his next meal was coming from. He stopped at a greasy spoon and ordered a full English, sitting by the window to get a feel for the area. A young woman walked past, pretty and carefree, and she grabbed his attention to the point he had the urge to fuck off his breakfast and follow her.

No, he couldn't. He had to stop this crap. Make a new start. What was it Lil had said? "If we stop doing shit that means we're bad, then it shows we're trying to make amends." He could do that if he tried hard enough. Go to a gym or something every time the need gripped him. It was just a habit, and they could be broken.

"I wonder what the coins mean. It's so specific…"

That had got Guv's back up big time. Only he knew what they meant, and he wasn't about to explain it to her. He'd made up an idyllic childhood, telling her all about it, because he was ashamed of how it had really been. He didn't even understand it himself, those coins and why he placed them there, so how would she? How odd, that a glimpse of those pennies on the floor as a child had stuck with him like that. Mum had entertained a lot of men as he'd been growing up, and this one bloke, he'd refused to hand over the required money. In the hallway, Mum had slapped the punter, pushed him, and he'd fallen arse over tit.

Laughing at her from the floor, he'd fished in his pocket and brought three coins out, saying, "This is all that was worth. You're shit in the sack." He'd placed them close, the edges butting together.

Guv had watched from between two banister rails on the stairs, and that incident, those coins, had cemented themselves in his head. No, Lil wouldn't understand. Especially because he left them for no reason he could fathom. None of the women were sex workers. Maybe he was telling himself they were *like Mum, dirty cows who opened their legs for anyone, so it justified him scaring the life out of them by moving shit about.*

"Weird that he rearranges what's in the fridge, though. There's got to be a reason for that an' all. Actually, do you remember you did that here when you first moved in? Said you couldn't find anything if it wasn't in order?"

Jesus, that had freaked him out. He'd fucked up there, setting her fridge up the way he liked it, the same as he had with the women. Back in his childhood, that fridge and where the contents were had been the only stable thing in his life. Everything else was so fucked-up and chaotic. Had Lil twigged he was the Stalker? Had she been testing him? That was another reason to get the fuck out of London sooner than he'd intended, because he had no doubt she'd have gone to Ron, and then Guv would be dead.

"I noticed you didn't pick up any strawberries *earlier."*

That had been it for him. She'd either followed him from the laundrette—and how fucking stupid of him to not have been more vigilant—or Ron had been keeping tabs on him by sending someone else to spy on him. He'd eaten a strawberry in Lacey Kopp's house, and someone had seen him. The same person Lil's mum had mentioned?

Whatever, that was behind him now, and he didn't have to think about it anymore. He could fake a good Mancunian accent, so he'd blend in with everyone else, find someone to settle down with. It wouldn't be the same, though.

She wouldn't be Lil, the woman he'd fallen in love with.

Chapter Twenty-Five

Fuming that he'd had to sit there and let George tie him up, Guv stared ahead at a blank TV. What the fuck did they do, watch soaps in between torturing people? He wouldn't give any of these three the satisfaction of looking them in the eyes, seeing his fear, especially not when he was frantically trying to work out how to get himself out of this mess. Saying that, he'd been left alone, so he had no one to avoid eye contact with anyway. What was this, they'd given him time to get really frightened, his brain going a mile a minute? Was it some kind of scare tactic?

He was used to Ron and his ways, how the big man had done it. Guv hadn't had a chance to really find out how the twins operated. Halibut had told him they were a nightmare, clever, and you didn't know where you stood with them half the time.

They were going to fuck with his mind, that much was obvious.

So… He'd been set up. Lil had done the dirty on him by going to The Brothers instead of dealing with this herself. He should have known she hadn't changed that much—the person she'd shown herself to be now was so different to the one he'd known all those years ago, and a leopard didn't change its spots. Well, not all of them. She'd lied in the pub, she *was* still a vindictive cow.

If she knew who he *really* was, she'd be fucking grateful he'd left London, pleased he'd never harmed her. She could have easily turned into one of his murdered women, although if he thought about it honestly, that was a massive lie. If Guv had ever hurt Lil and Ron found out it was him, he'd have been six feet under. Ron had a soft spot for her, putting the word out that if anyone hurt her, they'd have him to answer to.

Guv had soon decided to keep her as his cover.

He racked his brain to remember what had been said in the van on the way here—there had to be a clue there somewhere, but his head was groggy from that whack, and he couldn't grasp the whole conversation. Tendrils floated, and they'd have to be enough.

"You're in a whole world of shit, you arsehole." Had the twins found out he was the Stalker? And worse, that he'd become the Coin Creep? Or was this all happening because he'd left Lil without a word? An act of vengeance? Had George and Greg taken her sob story to heart, poor little laundrette woman abandoned, and they'd agreed to teach him a lesson?

If that was the case, then he'd walk out of here alive, or maybe drag himself out more like. If George stuck to his usual methods, he'd kneecap Guv. Maybe they'd banish him from London, and that wasn't such a bad thing. He'd started again in Manchester, and he could do the same anywhere else, although he'd just shelled out for the flat, so he'd lose money.

Losing money was better than losing your life, though.

"You lied to me the whole time we were together. I had no clue who you were." Why was he trying to kid himself? She knew. Which meant the twins knew. Fuck. There was no getting out of this except lying through his teeth. They couldn't prove he'd stalked and killed, otherwise the police would have done the same ages ago and picked him up by now. Guv had been careful not to leave any evidence behind that would point to him, so unless…

Shit, the camera at Avery's. Was that what had clued them in to it being him? Had the footage shown the top half of his face enough for them to have recognised him? They had a copper, that much was a given—had they found something out that way?

"I'll *be killing* you *soon…"* What was *that* all about? Were the twins handing her the reins? In a way, Guv reckoned he'd get off lightly if it was her ending him. She wasn't strong enough to strangle him, and he couldn't see her pulling a trigger or using a knife. So how did she plan to do it?

When they'd left him here, all of them had walked behind him, and one of the doors had opened and closed. Lil came back now, lingering in his peripheral. Was that a forensic suit? Guv thought back to beating that bloke up last night, George turning up all in white. It made sense, to safeguard themselves, to not rely on washing the bloodstained clothes, and there *would* be blood, they'd guarantee it. But maybe, if he could convince them all he was innocent, it would just be claret from a broken nose and a split lip.

Lil stood in front of him, her black leather gloves exchanged for the blue ones used in food prep. Rubber-like. Two more milk bottles appeared, taking up residence either side of her, and for a moment, because of the hoods pulled up, Guv couldn't work out which twin was which.

"Come on, you lot. What's this all about, eh?" Guv thought he'd sounded okay, not arrogant or anything. "If you could just tell me what's going on, we can clear up any misunderstanding."

"Who's Avery?" George asked.

Fuck. Bollocks. Keeping his face a straight mask, Guv said, "Who?"

"Don't fuck us about. Cut the crap and answer the question."

"I don't know any Avery."

George produced a phone and fiddled on the screen. He turned it round. Guv stared at a still image of him caught legging at across that fucking, pissing garden.

He remained impassive. "Who's that?"

George shook his head. "You're really taking the mick. What were you doing in her garden?"

"I wasn't in anyone's garden!"

"Right. So you didn't break into her house and wash up a cup and glass then put creepy music on an Alexa?"

Guv huffed out laughter, acting disbelieving. Or at least he hoped he came across that way. "You what?"

Lil turned to George, frowning. "Err, what's going on?"

Greg nudged her gently. "We said we'd explain, so we're explaining. Just listen." He focused on Guv. "Answer my brother before I kick your fucking head in."

Guv's brain whirred...*think, think!* "I have no idea how to use an Alexa because I've never owned one," he lied, "and why would I go into someone's house and wash up? It doesn't make sense."

"Who said it was a house?" George asked.

Guv rolled his eyes. "Okay, flat, maisonette, whatever."

"The next night, you did several things. You moved a toothbrush and paste. Knocked a shoe over. Turned a photo facedown. Opened the curtains, moved remote controls. Pissed about in the fridge."

"Oh no," Lil said.

"Put three coins on the hallway floor," George went on.

"Shit," Lil whispered. "Coins."

Guv laughed again. "Eh?"

George continued. "You took the lid off a casserole dish, propped it on a tub of margarine that's usually on a different shelf, and you opened a tin of beans and put a spoon inside it in the fridge. All subtle, all designed to be just enough to let your victim know someone's been in the house." He paced. "Now, correct me if I'm wrong, but these sorts of things happened in the

East End when you lived here, and when you left, they stopped. Then for the years you were in Manchester, they occurred again. You're known as the Coin Creep up there. Does it burn you that the press gave you such a shite name?"

"I don't know what you're on about."

"Yeah, you do." George's arm flashed out and struck him on the cheek, a proper backhander.

The pain stung. Guv blinked away the tears produced. "You've got the wrong bloke. I was here when that Stalker shit was going on, and I read about the Coin prick. You've got to be sick in the head to do anything like that."

"Hmm. Women died. Women who'd reported feeling like they were being watched, that someone had been in their houses and moved things. Why did some live and some die?"

"*I* don't fucking know, do I!"

George stopped beside Lil and stared. "Pax. Tell me about him."

How did they link that dickhead to me? Avery. They'd been to see her. "Who's that?"

"Ah, he's fucked up," Greg said.

"He has," George agreed. "See, we know you're aware of Pax because you fucking spoke to Jack about it in The Eagle, you div."

Guv went cold all over, goosebumps sprouting. He'd forgotten about that. "I spoke about the fire, yeah, but I didn't know his name was Pax."

"You got rid of him, broke his legs and burned the cunt to death because he might have caught you stalking Avery."

"What? I wouldn't burn *any*one!"

"Liar!" Lil spat. "I remember what you used to get up to for Ron, don't forget. You *have* set fires so people died. I *saw* you."

"No one died that night."

Lil smiled, but it wasn't a pleasant one. "I've got a picture of you standing in front of a burning gaff holding a petrol can. I took it with your fucking camera so I had something to hold over you if you ever stepped out of line with me. Ron would have dealt with you for me."

The betrayal stung even more than his cheek. She'd done that? Just what the hell had gone on between the old leader and Lil for there to be such a bond? Yes, they'd shagged, but why would Ron want to protect her so much? Did she have something on him? Or had Ron actually *loved* her?

"That was part of my job," he said. "But I wouldn't burn someone off my own bat."

George scoffed. "Were you jealous there was another stalker going around? Pax?"

"I had no idea that man was a stalker."

"We think you did. Was that why you beat up Eddie? So he'd be out of the picture and you'd be free to stalk Freya?"

"Who the fuck's Freya?"

George sighed. "This part of the conversation is boring me now. We know you were at Avery's, we know you killed Pax, and we know you're the one who's been terrorising women for years. *You* know that an' all. But what you *didn't* know, was the night you left, Lil was going to slice your face off."

Chapter Twenty-Six

Lil smiled at the shock on Guv's face. "I can see you're having trouble processing that. I'd put two and two together. I'd worked out you were the Stalker. I *followed* you to that *woman's* house. I thought Ron had worked it out, too. That's why, when you left, I assumed he'd banished you. Maybe even bumped you off. This Coin Creep shit is all news to me, but if it's you, it proves you can't control your urges or whatever the fuck they are. Why the need to stalk? Why kill some of them?"

"I'm not explaining myself because I can't."

George laughed. "He's fucked up again, bruv."

The Guv'nor blinked. "Shit."

"You may as well stop pretending," Lil said, "because no matter what you say, I'm going to kill you anyway. I've waited a long time for this." She turned to George. "Did you make my weapon for me?"

"I did." He pointed to the table.

She walked over there. A row of razor blades attached to pencils. George had used tiny screws to keep the blades in place instead of the glue and tape she'd used. "Why so many?"

"I wasn't sure if the pencils would snap, you know, when you get going. I used screws in case glue didn't hold up."

Lil collected her trusty little arsenal, held them behind her back, and returned to stand in front of Guv. "I loved you once."

Guv blinked. Seemed he'd loved her, too, going by his expression, his eyes watering.

"Fucking hell, Lil, I wanted it to work for us, but there was too much heat in London, the pigs were getting too close. I *had* to go."

George folded his arms. "Stealing a dead man's name isn't exactly the move of a genius, but it worked, didn't it, Reginald Noakes."

Guv closed his eyes—he knew he'd been caught good and proper. There was one thing Lil wanted the answer to, perhaps to try and understand Guv's reasoning. God knew *she* had reasons for doing what she had, for killing, but what were his? None of those women had hurt him, had they? They hadn't crossed the line and been rude to his mum.

And she thought about that, how she'd self-righteously propped herself up on such a weak excuse. She could admit now that it had just been a cover for her true nature—she was vindictive at heart, always had loved revenge, but she'd been a good person, too, the kindest at times. It would be difficult for some to understand how the two sides of her co-existed inside one person, and that was why she understood the twins, but mainly George. You *could* be good and bad at the same time yet be a decent person. Could that be applied to Guv?

"Why did you do it?" she asked.

Guv opened his eyes. Tried to stare into her soul, but she wouldn't let him. Those nights he'd done that, when they'd lain side by side in bed, she'd believed every word coming out of his mouth, sucked into his web of lies, but not today.

"I can't help myself. It's just inside me. The thrill of it. Scaring them."

"Did you know any of them? Did you make friends with them?"

"No, I followed birds about until the right one came along."

George huffed. "As in they lived alone."

"That was a factor, yeah." Guv took a deep breath. "I only killed them if they saw me. They were never supposed to see me, I fucked up the times they did, and I couldn't have them telling the police what I looked like."

Lil understood all that, how people's lives had to be ended if they posed a risk, but in these cases… Christ, they were innocent, pawns in his sick game. They weren't living in the seedy underbelly of gangland where the code was different and applied to them. Guv had stepped over into the other world, where the rules weren't the same, where those women didn't even know the rules existed.

"Everything you did is so wrong," she said. "You crossed a line." She brought her weapons out in front of her and handed all but one to George.

Guv stared at what she held, his frown showing how confused he was that it was a yellow HB pencil with a razor blade on the end.

"See this?" She held it up. "I've used something similar on two men before you and me got together. Slashed them up so bad their skin turned to ribbons. Ron stood and watched, then we got rid of their bodies together. My excuse was they upset my mum—no one was allowed to do that. Such a simple reason to end someone. I mean, I'm not right in the head to have taken such umbrage, to take it to such extremes, but it is what it is, and I own it. You were always good to her, you didn't mind me still living with her, and I'll thank you now for asking her out on dates with us, treating her nice with flowers and whatever. I was only going to kill you because I knew you were the Stalker."

"Your mum was a nice old bird."

"Yeah, she was. She'd have been so ashamed of me if she knew what I'd done. It was bad enough she found out I'd been seeing Ron, but she forgave me, loved me unconditionally. She was good like that. But I'm not. I can't forgive."

Lil stepped forward and swiped her arm up, the blade slicing him from jaw to temple in a diagonal. The skin on the bridge of his nose parted, blood pissing out of the deep cut in his cheek. She'd almost gone right through there. Guv screamed and scooted the chair back to get away from her, then stood, waddling off with the chair stuck to his back and arse. He headed for the main door. He must know he wouldn't get far, but his attempt at saving his life was instinctual and would be overriding common sense. He tried to bite the door handle and turn it, groaning at the pain that must have brought to his face.

"He'll give up in a minute," George said.

They all turned in a row to watch the spectacle.

"I really did care about him," she said. "Thought he was the one."

"I know, love." George put his arm around her. "But a cunt like that isn't good enough for you. I don't think there's many men out there who are."

She warmed at his words. Thought about what they'd been like as kids, those twins who'd run around like little bastards, stealing food for their mother to help her out, righting wrongs. And she thought about how proud Ron had been of them, despite hating the fact they were his sons. Contrary, he'd been, when it came to them. Did these lovely men know? Were they aware Richard wasn't their father?

"I can't seem to get any anger up," she said. "I thought I'd be raging, but…"

"It happens like that sometimes." George gave her a squeeze. "You spend years burning up with hatred, then when the time comes to get it all out of you, it doesn't happen. Want me to deal with him?" He held up the rest of the pencils.

Lil shook her head. "All those years I wasted, thinking about revenge when I could have been moving on with someone else. I can't even blame that on him, because it was all on me. I *chose* to think about killing him, I used it to get me through each day, something to focus on other than Mum being ill then dying. What the fuck will I entertain myself with once he's copped it?"

It worried her, not having something to occupy her, to stop her facing the grief that waited in the wings to claim her. She'd never let that grief in and sat with it because it would have been too painful. Instead, she'd gone to Elm House and sung, and every time she did, she pretended Mum sat in the corner, watching her, all proud, telling everyone, once again, that her daughter was amazing.

Tears stung, and a ball of what she recognised as grief threatened to expand and take over. She only ever allowed it to stay as a ball, but this time it seemed so much more insistent that she allow it to burst.

No, please don't come for me now. Not ever.

She ran forward, clutching the pencil, and reached a scrabbling Guv who headbutted the door as if that would open it. She grabbed the back of his hair and wrenched him away from it, her anger coming to her now, eclipsing that ball of mourning and creating a bomb instead. It exploded, her whole body going hot with rage, giving her the strength to drag Guv back to the twins. She shoved him away from her, and he staggered, falling onto his side. Lil hauled the chair upright, panting with the effort, and stared into his eyes.

She jabbed the razor into one of them, twisting, Guv's scream sounding distant where she'd gone into that headspace, the one from the past. She was underwater again, everything muffled, her softer emotions squashed into a box she couldn't access, only fury present, the need to hurt him. She yanked the blade out and hacked at his face, vaguely registering one of the twins going behind the chair and crouching, holding it steady. Lil's arm had a mind of its own, the pencil her baton as she conducted this orchestra, one she'd dreamed of for so long. Slice after slice after slice, his shoulders, his thighs, his shins, his dick. The pencil snapped, and she stood back, out of breath, taking in what she'd done.

Still underwater, she reached across and took the new pencil she instinctively knew was there, George's voice sounding far away.

"That's it, Lil, get all that poison out of you. Fucking have the bastard."

Ron, he'd sounded like Ron. It fired her up, those lethal words, and she hacked some more, bending to whip the blade over one of the hands that poked out from the bottom coil of rope. She moved to the other one, then bent to attack his feet, lifting one leg to score cuts into the soles, half severing his little toe. It happened as if everything was cushioned, her existence winnowed down to a bubble around her that flexed to accommodate her ever-moving arm. She rose and gripped the edge of Guv's ear, pulling it out then swiping from top to bottom, the ear coming off to another faint scream, although it would be loud if she stepped back into reality. Images of doing the same to Bod flashed up.

For now, she remained sheltered from her tender emotions by her brain keeping her safe from the horrors she committed, dulling them. She stuffed the ear into his gaping mouth. Removed as much of his nose as she could, stabbing the other eye. The second pencil broke, and she took a third from George, crisscrossing the blade over Guv's scalp, his lopped hair sliding down to land in the sticky blood on his shoulders. He raised his face to the ceiling, his unseeing, ruined eyes a fucking mess, and she took the final swipe.

His throat parted, blood coasting over his already scarlet skin, the many cuts, deep and shallow, and she *felt* the bubble fade as though it were real, as though Guv being dead was the green light for it to disintegrate. She wasn't ready for it to leave her, that cocoon, but it popped, thrusting her back into the real world where a man sat in front of her, every visible part of him ruined, blood on the floor in pools and spatters, bits of skin lying there as evidence of what she'd done.

For a second she mourned the fact the rope had kept some of him intact, but she had no more anger left to fix that. Lethargy infused her, seeping in until she felt so heavy she dropped the pencil and sank to her knees. A wave of 'what could have been' swept over her, taunting, telling her she'd never love anyone else and would be alone forever, always that woman who helped others, inserting herself into their lives like she'd done with Amy Osbourne.

"Deep breaths," George said. "That's it."

Greg rose from behind Guv and peered over. "Nice work. The state of his dick! Or what's left of it."

Lil fully came to, expecting to feel like she had before, righteous, justified, and it was so alien not to see Ron there, smiling at her, proud as punch that he'd encouraged the monster inside her to come out. But she felt nothing. Perhaps because this was the end of her mission, the thing that had supported her for so long—and knowing she had fuck all left to keep her centred and on track scared the shit out of her.

It was over, but she had a feeling the grief for Mum would win. It crept up on her now, and she panicked, drawing in huge lungfuls of air, her chest hurting.

"It'll be all right, I promise," George said. "We'll find something for you to do so it doesn't hurt so much."

He understood; he'd lost his mother, too.

She nodded, putting her trust in him. Her sanity. Because without a prop, she'd crumble, and Lil couldn't allow that.

Chapter Twenty-Seven

Flint stared at the screen of his perv laptop in shock. The London Teen landing page had changed. No login boxes, no 'sign up' banner, no Terms and Conditions tab. Just words. Words he couldn't wrap his head around. Big, bold letters in red. His skin, clammy, felt like it didn't belong to him. He wanted to claw it off as it heated up, as it tightened around his bones and muscles, an alive, foreign thing. His hot face burned so much it bordered on painful, itching. He read the words again, panic flouncing through him in the form of an over-ticking heart and lungs that seemed to have forgotten how to work.

THIS SITE IS TEMPORARILY CLOSED PENDING AN INVESTIGATION.

What did that even mean? What the *fuck* had happened? His mind went to the most obvious conclusion—it was a police investigation, and as the site was for teenagers, an adult infiltrator had been detected. He wasn't worried about getting caught because he used a VPN, but with his means of grooming removed, what the hell was he supposed to do?

He opened the files on his perv laptop, the one for the current girl. He scrolled through all the screenshots of their conversation so far, relieved he hadn't got to the proper grooming stage yet. They were still talking shit, the 'getting to know you' phase, and the most risqué thing he'd said was to ask for a shot of her tits. There was no way she'd have suspected he was a man and reported him. What about the ones before her?

He flicked through some other saved conversations, deeming himself safe from any repercussions. All of them had been too scared to dob him in. He opened the file for Summer Meeks/Mermaid, but she hadn't given him any reason to suspect she'd open her mouth either. She'd left all the money exactly where he'd told her to, then he'd closed down his username and started a new one.

Had Mermaid or any of the others broken down and told their parents? Or had some monitor or other on the site been scouring the private messages and had seen the grooming? It might not even be Flint they'd spotted. There had to be a load of other paedos on there.

To put his mind at rest, he scanned the last few interactions with Mermaid, him posing as Fishy_For_Life. No, there was nothing to worry about, she'd pleaded with him to believe she wouldn't say anything, that she'd keep the secret forever and:

MERMAID: PLEASE, PLEASE DON'T PUT MY PICTURES ON SOCIAL MEDIA.

Flint glanced at the clock. Fuck, he'd been staring at the screen for ages, losing track of time. He'd only nipped on to send a few love hearts to the latest girl before work, and now he was going to be late.

He wiped his history and cookies, closed the browser, and set the laptop to take it back to factory settings. Although what was the point? He knew how it worked, how things could be retrieved from the hard drive. A kernel of utter fright unfurled inside him. Something told him to ditch the fucking thing, just in case. Yeah, he'd do that later. Give himself a talking-to, go to therapy or some shit. Get help for his addiction.

He drove to work. Got out of the car. Janine Sheldon was just getting out of hers, too. She had a face on her, part annoyance, part contemplation. He blipped the key fob to lock his vehicle and jogged over to her.

"You all right?" He'd grown weirdly fond of her since she'd been teaching him how to work for the twins, something he'd never thought would be possible. She was a sour, abrupt cow who'd always given him dark looks. Now, though, he'd seen another side to her.

She grimaced. "No, I'm not all right as it fucking happens. This was meant to be my day off, but I've been called in."

"Murder, eh? Goes on more than people think."

"Yeah, well, this one might turn out to be a suicide if I'm lucky."

He knew what she meant, even though what she'd said sounded harsh, that suicide was anything to feel lucky about. "Yeah, then it's not your remit."

"Nope." She started off towards the station. "But I've been chosen as SIO until I can prove it isn't murder. The body's behind some trees in a kids' park, so that in itself looks dodgy."

Flint followed. "So who copped it or topped it, then."

She smiled at his dark humour. "I shouldn't find that funny, not when it's a child."

"Oh. Shit."

"Hmm." She pressed the code into the keypad to let them in. "And to answer your question, she's called Summer Meeks."

Flint's vision narrowed to a slice of the view in front of him, blackness crowding the edges: the door swinging open, Janine stepping inside then pausing to stare at him.

"You okay?" she asked, frowning.

Flint blinked. "What? Yeah. Just got a bit of a shock, that's all. Is she Terry's kid?"

"I think so. I haven't looked at the info yet, just got told who she was. I know Terry's been arrested a lot for being a dick in the pubs, but he doesn't deserve to go through this. I'm here to collect Colin, then we're going to the scene." She sighed. "Are you coming in or what?"

Flint got himself together and entered the station. Mermaid, dead. London Teens being shut down. He thought of his laptop and wanted to throw up. Wished he'd brought it with him so he could have disposed of it on the way here.

Janine walked off towards the stairs, and Flint made his way to the section where he worked. His legs had gone to jelly, so he dropped into his chair, propped his elbows on the desk, and put his face in his hands.

"Are you ill or something?" DC Kate Costa asked.

Flint raised his head. "Bad stomach."

"Then you shouldn't be here."

Flint rose, going to the DCI's office door and knocking. He had to get out of here, make out he was poorly. Get home and grab the perv laptop. Find somewhere to burn the bastard thing.

Vomit shot up and out of his mouth, splashing on the door.

"Oh, fucking hell, Flint!" Kate shouted. "You'd better clear that up, because I'm not doing it."

Piss off, you stupid fucking cow. Piss. Off.

Chapter Twenty-Eight

Lil had sent a message asking George and Greg to go to a cottage in the arse end of nowhere this morning. George had looked on Google Maps, and it was at the edge of a forest. It would make an ideal hideaway, secluded as it was.

"Wonder why she's asked us to go there?" Greg said from the driver's seat.

"Fuck knows, but something's up."

George didn't like not knowing, but Lil had decided to be mysterious, not only about the location but what she wanted to speak to them about. Ten minutes later, Greg pulled up outside and parked next to her Mini.

"Look at the windows." George gestured to them. Steel had been placed over the frames, the same with the door. "What the fuck?"

They got out of the van—George hadn't wanted to bring the BMW in case this was some kind of covert bollocks—and he hammered on the door. It opened, Lil standing there in a dressing gown and slippers, and she wandered down a hallway, going into a room on the left.

George and Greg followed, finding her in a pretty decent lounge, even if it was a bit dated. She sat on a black leather sofa, legs tucked to one side on the seat next to her. A tall lamp stood in the corner, lighting the room in the absence of sun coming through the windows. It was a bit weird that curtains hung as though the steel outside didn't exist.

"Take a seat." She gestured to the other sofa.

The twins sat, and George raised his eyebrows for her to get the fuck on and explain herself.

"Don't rush me," she snapped. "I've been wrestling with whether to tell you about this place. It's the first time I've been back in years."

She'd already told them her story, but it seemed not all of it if he was any judge. Maybe not revealing everything had been playing on her mind.

She picked at a fingernail. "I'm going to preface this by telling you I know who you are."

George stared at her. "Eh?"

"Ron was your father—unless that was another fucking lie he told me."

George hid his anger and laughed. "Err, that's a lie, yes."

"I should have known. That man was such an arsehole. All these years I've been thinking I've kept a secret, not only for him but for your mother, and I needn't have bothered."

"What's all this about, Lil? Not being rude, but we've got somewhere to be. Terry Meeks' kid's dead, and we need to pay a condolence call."

"Fine, we'll do this another time."

"No, we're here now." Greg nudged George's knee with his.

Lil sighed. "Not many people know this, but Ron had multiple affairs. His wife had no clue, neither did the majority of people, but a few of us did. We never said anything, of course, we let him think he was fooling everyone, but he was a nasty player, and I happened to fall for his charm."

George sucked in a breath. "Right..."

"I knew what I was walking into, but it didn't work out like all the others. For a start, I was seeing him for months, and he signed this place over to me, bought my Mini, kitted out the laundrette. Reckoned he loved me—that's debateable—but anyway, I'd have done anything for him until...until I didn't want to anymore. It's funny, but I got away with talking to him like shit, and he never did anything to hurt me because of it. Anyway, we split up, and I moved on. Got with Guv. Before that, though, I had two other fellas. Both of them are dead now because I killed them. Jake and Bod, the ones I told you about. Jake used to knock me about, and I never passed that on to Ron at first because he'd chosen him for me."

"Chosen?" George frowned.

"Long story short, but Ron had to let me go because he was getting in too deep with me, or so he said, so he picked Jake as a replacement. Anyway, it all went sour, and the three of us ended up here." She glanced over at the door. "What I assume used to be the dining room is covered all round in steel. There's a trapdoor in the floor. Ron strung men up with chains, killed them, and let them fall into the space beneath the cottage. He used to go down there and shift them around, make more room. God knows how many bodies are there. Mind you, they'd be skeletons by now."

Greg glanced at George: *How did we not know about this? We followed him umpteen times in the van.*

George shrugged in response.

Lil stopped picking her nail and stuffed her hands beneath her armpits. "I don't think anyone but me knows this, but Ron was a bit of a lone wolf sometimes. He said he missed who he used to be, going one-on-one with people, so he'd go out, round someone up, and bring them here."

Greg raised his eyebrows at George: *Remind you of anyone?*

Yeah, George had a phase of going out as his Ruffian self, but it wasn't because he wanted a one-on-one experience. Not in the same way as Ron anyway. George had wanted to find out what it was like to not be a twin, to be his own person instead of one of a pair. He'd enjoyed it but soon realised he was better off running around with Greg. Still, it naffed him off that he had something in common with his real father.

"We'd have brought Guv here if he hadn't fucked off," she said. "I should have got hold of Ron as soon as it became clear Guv was the Stalker, but I got it into my head that I wanted to confront Guv about it, sort it myself. If I'd opened my mouth, none of those women in Manchester would be dead, the other half frightened out of their minds that they're still being watched. And now, with Guv dead, those women will never know they're safe. And that's all on me."

"You can't carry *all* the blame," George said.

"I can't see myself shaking out of this. I came here last night, slept over, thinking I could put a lot of things to bed, but all it's done is dredge up memories. But there's one thing good that can come out of it. Look, I know there's dead blokes under the floor, but I want you to use this gaff however you need to. It could do with being updated if you're going to let people stay the night, but there's no damp, I've kept the heating on low every winter, paid all the bills, that sort of thing. But I don't want it. I can't come here again, and I can't exactly sell it, can I, what with the steel room and the bodies."

"That room would come in handy," Greg said. "We could use the place as somewhere to hold people, and Will can sleep over to keep an eye on them instead of doing it at the warehouse."

"That doesn't happen often," George said, "but I see what you mean. I could get a few new tools, keep them here. Have a good old torture session then cart the bodies to the warehouse for cutting up and disposal." He looked at Lil. "You okay with that?"

"I'd say like father like son, but you've already said that's bullshit."

She was grinding his gears, but he wouldn't let her know it. "Unfortunately, we're stuck with Richard as our father, and no amount of suspicion on your part is going to change that. In a way, Ron would be the better option, but ah well." He stood. "So you're all right with us gutting this place and getting a new kitchen and bathroom, decent furniture and whatever?"

"Yep, do whatever you like. There's a spare set of keys on the hallway table. I'll lock up after I leave. You can collect mine from the laundrette when you're next passing."

Greg got up and went to get them.

George looked down at her. "Sorry you went through so much shit in life, Lil."

She smiled. "Some of us are destined to fight against the tide. I'm used to it."

"Maybe now you've got everything off your chest you can move on."

"Nice sentiment, but unlikely. Now fuck off. I need a good cry and don't want an audience."

Chapter Twenty-Nine

Two Weeks Later

She hadn't expected to be asked to do a job like this, but it was one she'd always dreamed of. More of a detective role than being out there on the streets. PC Anaisha Bolton had set up her username on London Teens. While the site had been down, the owner, Brandon Cox, had brought in a specialist who'd discovered some users opted to access the site via VPNs, which masked their home or work IPs, instead presenting as one that was a VPN endpoint. Brandon had come in to explain that to the Internet Crimes team working on catching whoever Summer Meeks had been speaking to.

Two endpoints created a private connection, which was what the London Teen site registered as the user. However, if that VPN IP address was a known one, which some of them were, then sites knew their users were coming in under protection. Other times, they didn't, when the VPN was completely masking them. In the case of the user who'd been chatting to Summer, the endpoint IP was known.

For now, the team had called the person Unknown.

Anaisha's head had hurt from all the jargon, but she understood it now. In simple terms, whoever had spoken to Summer/Mermaid was one of two people using the same VPN, so her job of luring in the man—or woman—would be easier. For now, she chatted on the forum, hoping to God she came across as young. She was, at twenty-two, and acting immature was proving easier than she'd thought.

Based on the proof on Summer's laptop that she'd sent photos to Unknown, a lot of them naked, Anaisha had called herself Loves_Risqué_Shots. If that didn't draw the perverted bastard in, she didn't know what would. Sadly, all private messages on the server were encrypted, so Brandon hadn't been able to provide evidence that Unknown had spoken to other girls. Bloody stupid, when the site was full of vulnerable kids. More intel on Summer's laptop had narrowed down some specifics, though, and thank God the team had access to it.

He preferred no makeup. He didn't like big breasts.

She felt icky about the prospect of being spoken to as if she were a child. Her profile stated she was thirteen, wished she had bigger boobs—BEING FLAT-CHESTED SUCKS! she'd added—and she loved flirting. Her only worry was that he only chose white girls, which was something she'd brought up in one of the team meetings last week. If she sent him her photo and he saw she was of black and white ethnic heritage, would he reject her? All this planning would have been for nothing, then.

She spent the next hour on a thread with the title: WHO'S YOUR FAVOURITE SINGER? That subject wasn't difficult, so she mentioned a few stars the kids were into these days, checking Google to make sure she got things right. Just as she was about to claim she loved old-school music, too, her private message alert pinged. Her heart thumped, and she raised her arm and circled her hand to let her colleagues know someone had contacted her and they needed to come over.

They gathered round, everyone's focus on the screen.

She opened the message box.

AMATEUR_PHOTOGRAPHER: HEY!

LOVES_RISQUÉ_SHOTS: HEY, HOW ARE YOU DOING?

AMATEUR_PHOTOGRAPHER: GREAT. YOU?

LOVES_RISQUÉ_SHOTS: I'M GOOD. WHAT ARE YOU UP TO?

AMATEUR_PHOTOGRAPHER: BORING HOMEWORK.

LOVES_RISQUÉ_SHOTS: SAME.

AMATEUR_PHOTOGRAPHER: GOT ANY PICS?

LOVES_RISQUÉ_SHOTS: GOD, TALK ABOUT GETTING STRAIGHT IN THERE. I'LL SEND ONE, BUT ONLY IF YOU SHOW ME YOURS, TOO.

His dropped immediately. A photo came up of a boy of around fifteen.

"Do a Google reverse image thing," Oliver said.

"Hang on, I'd better send him mine first." Anaisha had uploaded several pics from her teenage years, but a DC who was a wizard on Photoshop had made them look more recent.

*IMG_000_12

LOVES_RISQUÉ_SHOTS: I'M RUNNING AWAY TO HIDE NOW.

Anaisha downloaded the one he'd sent and did an image search. It came up on several stock sites and could be purchased for a few quid.

"It's him, got to be," Oliver said. "If he was genuine, it'd be a photo off his phone."

AMATEUR_PHOTOGRAPHER: DON'T HIDE. YOU'RE BEAUTIFUL. LOVE A GIRL WITHOUT MAKEUP. YOUR USERNAME…ARE YOU LYING?

LOVES_RISQUÉ_SHOTS: NOPE. I HAVE A FEW PICTURES THAT WOULD MAKE YOUR EYES POP OUT, BUT I DON'T KNOW YOU, SO YOU'RE NOT SEEING THOSE.

AMATEUR_PHOTOGRAPHER: LOL. DON'T BLAME YOU. CAN'T BE TOO CAREFUL. THE INTERNET'S FULL OF PERVS.

LOVES_RISQUÉ_SHOTS: GOD, YOU SOUND LIKE MY DAD.

AMATEUR_PHOTOGRAPHER: HAHA!

LOVES_RISQUÉ_SHOTS: SHIT, I'VE GOT TO GO. MUM'S CALLING ME FOR DINNER.

AMATEUR_PHOTOGRAPHER: OKAY. CHAT LATER? OR TOMORROW?

LOVES_RISQUÉ_SHOTS: YEAH. [HEART EMOJI]

"Perfect," Oliver said. "Fucking well done, girl."

Anaisha smiled, chuffed to bits with the praise.

If Unknown turned out to be Amateur_Photographer, aka Fishy_For_Life, then they were in with a chance of finding him if she played her cards right. Summer had killed herself from shame, she'd sent her mum and dad an email that had been set on a delayed send. Anaisha would do everything she could to get justice for her.

She stared at the chat, grossed out that he could be perving over her photo right this second. She'd never understand men like him.

Enjoy me while you can, fucker, because I'm gunning for you.

To be continued in *Readies*,
The Cardigan Estate 30

Printed in Great Britain
by Amazon

41824336R00209